The Organ Thief

by

Kenneth B. Chamberlin

Second Edition

D1490477

PUBLISHER'S NOTE:

This work is a medical fiction, a genre that aspires to truth in fiction. Places are all geographically correct, while characters and incidents are a product of the author's imagination. Locales and public names are sometimes used for atmospheric purposes. Any resemblance to actual people, living or dead, or to businesses, companies, events, institutions, or locales are completely coincidental. This book is intended for your entertainment and enjoyment.

ACKNOWLEDGEMENT

I would like to thank my spouse for her dedicated editing efforts on this novel, which I appreciate very much. I also thank my sister Ardythe for reading the final draft and offering her valued spelling skills. Without their assistance and encouragement, this book would not be in your hands to read.

Kenneth B. Chamberlin

Table of Contents

Chapter 1

DONOR BANK DEPOSIT

Dr. **Collin MacDonald** stood in his private operating room in the basement of his rural Boston home. It was a two-story building, set back from the cul-de-sac, on a treed one-acre lot. Like the other six neighboring homes, a circular driveway off the cul-de-sac provided access to the house. His neighbors appreciated the care and attention the doctor lavished on the property's spacious flower gardens and shrubbery.

Originally, the property was quite flat and mundane in appearance. He had hired a few laborers to excavate the crawlspace to create a play area for his children in the basement. The excess soil was used to contour the front and back lawns.

After his family died, Collin seemed to take a greater interest in landscaping the property. He dug and spread ash into the lawn to enrich the soil, then planted a variety of Begonias, Geraniums and shrubs. His large colonial home was bordered on each side by giant cedar trees, nestled amongst small mounds of soil. The white house with its dark window-sashes and matching trim, gave it the appearance of a country estate.

His medical operating theater was located in the converted basement. It was equipped with all the tools he needed to maintain his new, thriving business venture. It had not always been like this, just for the past few months, since he lost his family.

Today he was in a hurry. A pair of kidneys were urgently needed, as well as a large quantity of full-thickness skin-grafts. The not-so-willing donor was type O-negative and her harvested parts would be compatible with all blood type recipients.

He wore a clear plastic-sleeved hospital gown of his own design that covered his body completely. Surgical gloves, face shield and mask completed his ensemble. All that was visible of his middle-aged Scottish face were the brown eyes and the heavy dark eyebrows.

As he rolled the unconscious woman onto her stomach, he noted the muscle tone and firmness of her body. It was a shame to waste such a fine specimen for the few organs requested by his contact this morning. He would have to email his broker, who worked for the National Organ Donors Transplant waiting list, to see if more harvested items could be used.

He cut the carotid arteries in her neck and allowed the blood to flow into the catch basin below the stainless-steel table. The blood would be flushed down the floor drain when he had finished the operation.

After washing the back, buttocks and legs with Povidone-iodine and Isopropyl alcohol, Collin shaved the hair from the cleansed areas. Using an electrical dermatome, he carefully removed strips of the flesh and blood vessels, in addition to the top two layers of skin from the donor. These he washed in saline and stored them in labeled airtight containers. The labels included the donor's ID, donor site location, tissue and blood type, age, sex and race.

With a little nutrient media added to help maintain the tissue, it was placed in the refrigerator at 4 degrees Celsius. The small amount of blood still flowing from the warm donor's body was directed into the catch basin where water was added before the fluid drained into the city storm sewage system.

With the allogenic skin-graft complete, Collin now concentrated on removal of the kidneys. As he didn't expect to use much more from this donor, he simply cut the body apart, just above the hips with his bone-saw to remove the two organs. These were bagged and placed in a bed of ice for shipping. He then placed the two body halves in a tub and poured fifty pounds of ice cubes from his commercial ice machine over the naked body. It would keep until later that evening when he returned. He now had an appointment to keep with the distributor of his valuable commodity.

He removed his soiled plastic gown and the rest of his surgical gear and placed them with the body halves. He then collected his rolling organ-cooler containing the organs and walked to the small elevator at the front of the room. This hidden elevator transported him to the first-floor coat-closet. No one knew about his elevator, hidden within the cedar-lined closet that he had originally built to store visitor's coats. At the back of the closet, there was a secret panel that opened the elevator door. The conveyance was just large enough to fit himself and a hospital gurney.

En route to his **rendezvous** with Sid Fournier that December evening, Collin recalled their first meeting in 2005. Collin had finished his internship at Boston Mass. Hospital and was a practicing surgeon at the hospital. One of his patients, a diabetic elderly lady, was in desperate need of a kidney and pancreas transplant. She was the favored aunt of Sid Fournier, a young attorney, practicing estate and property-transfer law.

Aunt Gladys had been on the waitlist for several years and the prognosis for her survival was not good. Sid had pulled every imaginable string in his search for a matching donor kidney. He was, at long last, rewarded when a fellow told him that an organ could be available if the money was right. Jumping at the opportunity without much forethought or consideration for legalities, Sid paid the fellow the inordinate asking price of $25,000.00 in unmarked bills. The organ was slotted into the National Organ Donor (NOD) supply pipeline. Four hours later, as promised, a uniformed courier from the NOD delivered a small portable cooler, addressed to Mass. Hospital, care of Dr. Collin MacDonald, Re - Gladys Fournier.

Dr. MacDonald had been given little more than two hours' notice that a donor with type A+ blood had died.

The paperwork accompanying the organ reported the deceased was from a Women's Hospital west of Boston. A pancreas and kidney for Gladys with type AB+ blood was en route.

Her family gathered at the hospital.   Cousins, siblings and nephews, including the young attorney, Sid Fournier. All of them were intent on celebrating Aunt Glady's good fortune.

The kidney with the pancreas still connected to the small intestine through a tube, called the pancreatic duct, was transplanted into Gladys. The operation took four-hours to complete. She had been a longtime sufferer of type 1 diabetes. While she was being moved to Recovery, Dr. MacDonald attended the family in the waiting room. He announced the good news and cautioned that all was not perfect. There was the possibility that elderly lady might reject this kidney. If her condition worsened, she could require a new kidney in the future. She would have to reduce her sugar intake and watch her diet closely.

Sid had an envelope with a thank-you card signed by the family that he passed into the doctor's hand. While the family celebrated, Collin slipped the envelope into his pocket and left the room. Once he arrived at the

Surgeon's Lounge, Collin tossed the unopened envelope containing the thank you card onto the top shelf of his locker. It would remain there for over a year.

When Collin eventually found the envelope, he discovered five new one-thousand-dollar bills inside with a thank-you note. A business card belonging to the young attorney was included with a note suggesting Dr. MacDonald contact the writer, if he wanted to earn a few extra dollars.

Ten years went by before Collin re-connected with the young lawyer. In the meantime, he put the much-needed $5,000 to good use. He hired a crew of laborers to excavate the crawlspace under his recently purchased home in Newton Highlands to construct a basement play area for his two children.

Collin had married his college sweetheart in 2004, the last year of his internship and they became parents in the first 18 months of their marriage, to a boy and a girl. There was little time for leisure during those days of changing diapers and 2:30 a.m. bottle-feedings. They were a happy couple, who enjoyed planning the renovation to their Newton Highlands home.

Collin was 6'-2" and his once athletic frame cried out for exercise. His profession as a surgeon dictated long hours bent over a patient, inserting or removing body parts while wearing magnifying goggles. Microscopic suturing of blood vessels and tissue require both precision and stamina. Surgeries of this nature can often take 10 hours to complete so the last thing he wanted to do after one of these operations, was exercise or work on his home renovations. He wasn't overweight, just out of shape and was not in peak condition.

The couple wanted to build a recreation room as an addition to the existing basement which was just under 400 sq. ft. It was just large enough for the HVAC heat-pump system, hot water tank and washer/dryer. Tracy wanted additional space in the basement for the children to play. As it was now, she could not hear the children playing upstairs when she did the laundry in the basement.

She was a petite woman at 5'-4", whose features were perfectly proportioned. Barbie-doll replica came to mind when Collin saw her for the first time. She had little need for makeup or jewelry to adorn her body or draw attention to herself. Tracy was confident and strong-willed. These were traits she had inherited from her father, a US Marine Sargent who had been killed in Vietnam in 1967.

Their children, two-year old Donald and almost three-year old Sylvia were growing quickly, while the work on the recreation room progressed slowly. Sylvia thought she might be a parent herself before the basement construction job would be completed. Access was still via the stairs and through the laundry room. The rec-room was primarily designated as a playroom for the children and their friends. There were no windows because the original house sat on a concrete slab at grade. Ventilation was supplied by tapping into the heating and air conditioning ductwork. The view to the rest of the neighbors gave no hint of any livable space beneath the house.

Collin had put his study in the far corner so he could keep an eye on the children's activities. Not counting the laundry room, the children had over 1,000 square feet to run and play in. With the extra insulation in the ceiling, their screeching voices could barely be heard upstairs. Tracy left the door to the basement open when they played down there, and Collin had installed a closed-circuit TV with the monitor in the kitchen.

The family enjoyed their rural lifestyle and the children made friends easily at school. Their mother Tracy had become friends with every neighbor for three blocks in all directions. The family was kept busy, attending numerous functions around the Newton Highlands area.

Tracy volunteered as a Teacher's Aide twice a week and Collin volunteered as an Assistant Soccer Coach when time allowed. Every Tuesday he attended a men's-only poker game, held at a different home each week. The seven players had been friends since college. They had been getting together for twelve years now to play Texas Hold'em. Meanwhile, Tracy went to a yoga session and then had cocktails with the girls on those nights. A neighbor's teenage daughter came to babysit, and the kids loved the change.

While the MacDonald family thrived happily, the last child, a girl they named Emma was born after a seven-year interval.

Life, as they knew it, ended in a split-second one rainy evening in July 2015. On their way home from a birthday party, a drunk driver in his pickup truck, t-boned their vehicle on the passenger side doors. Collin's wife Tracy and their son Donald were killed instantly. Emma, the infant, although strapped snugly in her car-seat in the middle of the backseat, suffered massive, internal bleeding and died two days later. Their eldest,

Sylvia, who sat behind Collin, was crushed and went into a coma as did Collin. Collin awoke three weeks later. His daughter Emma remained in a vegetable state for another four weeks before her life-support was terminated.

While Collin and his daughter were in a coma, the other family members were put into refrigeration to await Collin's recovery. There was no Will or instruction of any sort found by the police when they searched the family's home. The children's grandparents were deceased and there were no parental siblings to take control or make decisions while Collin was comatose.

When he regained consciousness, Collin was devastated by the loss of his family. Only Sylvia remained. She was in a coma and with little probability of survival. His wife and two dead children's usable organs had degraded by the weeks of refrigeration in the hospital's morgue.

Collin saw to the cremation of his family and watched over his daughter's frail small body as it withered away before his eyes. She was connected to life-support, without brain activity. While Medical standards dictated that she was dead, Collin held on, praying to God for a miracle, to no avail. He saw to the needs of others by consenting to donate every conceivable part of his daughter for transplants. There was but a small container of her remains to inter with the rest of the family's ashes.

Collin was inconsolable in his deep and lonely grief. Once he recovered from his broken ribs and severe concussion, he tried to restart his life. He returned to work for a few days but couldn't cope with the suffering of others. The images he saw, whenever he closed his eyes, was the two-ton GMC truck charging through the red light, straight into his family's minivan. The sound of the crushing, tearing metal during the collision kept reverberating in his mind. The drunk driver ran from the crash-site without aiding any of the MacDonald family. He was caught eight blocks away in a tavern, having a few shots of bourbon to settle his nerves. Blood was still seeping from the only injury he sustained, a cut to his left ear caused by his seatbelt.

Collin rattled around the family home in Newton Highlands, unable to eat, neglecting to care for himself, unshaven and needing a bath. His world was over. He could see no escape from the depressing pain of losing of his young family.

His poker buddies tried to console him. The neighbors came by with pot pies, casseroles and soups. Even the local Protestant Minister stopped in to visit, despite the MacDonald's not having been church members. Mail from insurance companies, the repair shop where Tracy's minivan was stored, along with dozens of cards and letters of condolence went unopened. Collin never wanted to see his wife's car again. He wanted to be free of the world and its painful reminders of his loved ones.

Then one day, about three months after the accident, Collin quietly rejoined the living and snapped out of his desperation. He shaved off his beard, got cleaned-up, put on his best suit and returned to work. He put his shoulder to the wheels of the Mass. Hospital's surgical team and worked as if there was no time for anything else. No one knew why or what had pulled him from his grief. None dared ask, for fear of re-triggering his grief.

Collin's daughter Sylvia had come to him in a dream. She told him there was a need for his help. She urged him to find the thank-you card and to resume his surgical service to the community. He did not tell a soul about the dream. He decided to heed his daughter's advice to retrieve the card of thanks from the Fournier family.

His mind cleared as he recalled the kidney transplant operation, he had performed on Aunt Gladys ten years earlier. That memory moved Collin to finally see his way out of the darkness. It was his eureka moment, his perfect solution to the donor-organ shortage that kept so many lives of the desperately ill in limbo.

To put his plan into action, he would first need to re-establish his income and organize a short list of associates willing to support his idea. Then he would set up a private, secure medical operating theater and laboratory.

Collin had soon worked out the details of his organ-donor network. He found loopholes that would enable him to insert healthy organs into the National Organ Donor system without detection. He then called Sid Fournier, to arrange a meeting at Collin's home for the very next week in November 2016. His invitation to the lawyer had briefly mentioned an unlimited source of money.

"Good evening Sid, thank you for making time for me on such short notice," Collin said. Taking Sid's overcoat, he hung it in the newly built cedar-lined closet in the entrance foyer.

"Come, let's sit in the library, where we can take advantage of the wet-bar on this cold winter's eve," Collin said. "What's your pleasure, Sid?"

"Scotch neat, one ice cube," came the reply.

"Now tell me, Dr. MacDonald, what is this all about?

"I like the unlimited funds you mentioned. Now tell me, what's the rest of the story?" Sid asked.

"By all means, let me explain it to you. First, please call me Collin. If we are to collaborate in this business plan of mine, we will need to trust each other. That trust comes from being close as well as truthful," Collin said.

"Alright Collin, I agree that trust and full disclosure are paramount in a partnership. Now, what's on your mind?" Sid asked.

"Since the time of your aunt's kidney and pancreas replacement, obtaining donated organs has become much more difficult. People die in the thousands every year in the United States and their organs die with them. You discovered that yourself, when you had to buy a kidney for your aunt on the black market. I believe I have an organ source that will help alleviate this problem. Our Congress continues to pass laws to restrict how, who and when a person can donate their organs. While donors are quite willing, hospitals and clinics won't remove organs if it is illegal to do so", Collin explained.

"Iran permits an open-market exchange of organs and so should the USA. In Iran, a person can legally sell their own kidney or part of a lung to the state for the benefit of another. Relatives are permitted to sell the organs of their deceased family members. The state transplants the organs and assists living donors who have health issues for as long as necessary. In China, dead prisoner's organs are all donated. Neither of these countries have waiting lists for transplantable organs.

In America, a prisoner condemned to death by lethal injection must lay undisturbed for 15 minutes until a doctor checks the heart and officially declares the prisoner dead by lethal injection. This delay causes serious concern due to hypoxia destruction of the organs. However, if organs are removed any earlier, the cause of death would be deemed "removal of organ" rather than "lethal injection". It is a quandary and lawmakers have not yet found a solution.

"What is needed is an operating theater outside of the strict controls of our Congress. We need a clinic for terminal donors so that their organs can be preserved and donated. The citizens of our country want this relaxation of procedures and I want to provide the service. Now that you've heard the gist of my ethical but somewhat illegal proposal, what do you think?" Collin asked.

"I think that organs donated from willing, live donors will not be sufficient to satisfy our needs, regionally or nationally. How do you intend to recruit donors?" Sid asked.

"I plan to advertise by word of mouth, not through the media. I will connect with morgues and crematoriums. You would be surprised how many professional people are opposed to the strict rules of government controls in the sale of organs," Collin said.

"It won't be long before we are turning away customers. Are you interested in joining me in this venture? Your end would be the organ distribution into the donor pipeline and fee collection."

"That question is like asking if the Pope is Catholic. You can be assured that I'm in, up to my eyebrows and then some! When can we get this distribution network operating?" Sid asked.

"Soon. Come with me. I'll show you the operating room I've built in the basement."

Collin led his guest down the stairs into the laundry room, past the children's play area. It was on the street-side of the basement that he had converted.   A cinderblock wall ran down the center of the basement play area lengthwise, giving him an 18 ft. x 40 ft. clinic area.

"Over here is the laboratory, complete with a centrifuge, microscope, autoclave, and all the essential tools," Collin explained. "I even have an ice-cube maker for ice to pack the organs with," Collin said. "I can do complete blood work-ups here and I plan to have DNA-identifying equipment, when my financial resources improve."

"Perhaps I can invest a few dollars on my end to increase my profit share," Sid offered. "That is a substantial-looking operating table. It looks more like an autopsy table." Sid said.

"I bought what I could find without too many questions. I plan to use a rubber-covered operating cushion on the table for the patient's comfort. There will be a wash sink in that corner and TV cameras will be installed at the operating table to film the surgeries for live donor patients," Collin concluded.

He was not about to tell Sid about the crematorium oven he planned to install on the other side of the cinderblock wall. It would be part of the pottery hobby he planned to have in the play area. It would have an exhaust scrubber to clean the smoke it generated before sending it up the first-floor fireplace chimney. The secret entrance via the elevator from the hall closet was also kept from Sid. For security reasons, the less Sid knew about Collin's renovations and equipment, the better. He predicted he would get at least ten-years out of this arrangement before the police got even close to discovering it.

The two men shook hands and returned to the library to finalize the terms of their new partnership. Upon Collin's insistence, they should never meet in person again. He explained how to use an unsecure Wi-Fi system to send coded messages via the internet. Funds would be deposited into offshore bank accounts. In emergency situations, they would communicate using a cheap burner cell phone, destroying it and the SIM-card after each call. Collin gave his new partner a dozen burner phones acquired over the past weeks from small corner stores. They each had twenty-minutes airtime and Collin kept a list of the phone numbers.

If ever they were questioned by the authorities, they were to acknowledge that they had initially met through aunt Gladys. They would both recall that their last meeting was a condolence visit, one cold evening in November. That alibi was devised in case a neighbor's security camera might have identified Sid's car in Collin's driveway.

Sid left later that evening, feeling a sense of kindness in his heart for the great service he was about to bestow on the citizens of Boston. Too bad it had to be kept a secret, he thought to himself as he drove home on #9. He would write his own diary of events and perhaps someday, it might make a great novel. A story about a humanitarian surgeon and an estate lawyer, collaborating to do good for society. That would be his own little secret.

Chapter 2

DONOR FISHING TRIP

Collin's first use of his new laboratory was to brew up a flask of clear Gamma Hydroxybutyric Acid, better known as GHB or date rape drug. When used in a cocktail, it doesn't discolor or change the taste of the drink. Newer, commercially available drugs, such as Ketamine had subtle tastes, while some had LSD-type side effects. GHB was perfect for Collin's needs. It was a little salty but unnoticeable in a sweetened drink. A victim could be under his control in just 15 minutes and would remain that way for 3 or 4 hours. Once it wore off, the drug was undetectable in the major organs or the blood stream of the victim. A pathologist, looking for it shortly after it was suspected to be present, could find traces but Collin's victims would be dead by that time.

Armed with his vial of GHB, Collin made his way to the seedy side of East Boston, one of several to be found in the city. Collin's first visit was to the Dutchman's Bar on a side-street off Arlington, in an area known as Eastie.

When Collin entered the bar, he was met with a wet-dog smell, often prevalent in rundown drinking establishments. There were water stains on the ceilings and walls and a musky smell permeated everything. The low lighting and music lulled the few patrons into forgetting just how decrepit and rundown the place was.

The lone barmaid had more piercings in her eyebrows and ears than her gramma's pincushion. A small, silver box-chain, drooped from her right ear and connected to her nostril. Her exposed skin was decorated in a multitude of tattoos. *She would not make a good candidate as a skin-graft donor,* Collin thought to himself.

Four men sat at the corner of the bar; each was nursing various alcoholic drinks. They were a rough-looking group of men, dressed in construction work clothes. They all wore toques and hoodies, not as fashion statements but rather to ward off the cold mid-December night. Further along the bar, away from the door, two women sat by themselves with three empty bar stools between them.

The six booths along the east wall held groups of similarly dressed patrons. Their heads were nearly touching during their whispered conversations in the darkened bar. Two punks, wearing shirts with torn-off sleeves to emphasize their biceps, attempted to played pool. They tried to look tough for the three girls who watched and giggled at the table next to the toilet doors.

With a watchful eye for detail, Collin moved to the empty end of the bar, furthest from the entrance door. He blended in easily with his dockside wool pea-coat and toque. Surveying each patron, he picked out two that he pre-qualified as potential organ donors. They had shooter glasses in front of them and a glazed, distant look in their eyes. The one closest to him was a woman of about thirty-five, slim, about 112 lbs. She was poorly dressed for the weather but provocatively, to attract potential customers.

The second candidate sat in a booth with what looked to be his son, arguing over some family matter they wished to keep secret. The father appeared to be drunk and he slurred his words in an effort to speak eloquently. He badgered the boy, insisting that it was too early to return home.

The blue haze of cigarette smoke hung at shoulder height, since everyone in the room except Collin smoked. The father smoked plain cigarettes and the woman Collin was interested in at the bar, smoked a menthol filtered type. Mentholated cigarettes some people believed, were healthier for them.

Collin sipped his bottled beer as he just couldn't persuade himself to drink out of a glass in this filthy, smog-layered place. He watched the pool game but kept track of his two-donor fish. Tonight, was a practice run. He was testing the water on his quarries' habits and the reaction of the other patrons in the bar. He wanted a DNA sample, to learn the person's name and whether they frequented the bar regularly. It was catch and release, for now, on this cold December evening.

In Collin's mind, all people who got drunk in public were potential drunk drivers, just like the one who had taken his family from him. He considered them no better than garbage, disposable and useless with one exception. They could serve society by providing desperately needed transplant organs.

"May I buy you each a drink in the spirit of the Christmas season? I'll be heading home in the morning for the holidays, to be with my wife and kids. This is my last night in Eastie until after Christmas," Collin said. He had turned slowly toward the two women near him in a nonthreatening way. Giving him the once-over to ensure he was harmless, the two nodded their acceptance.

"Do you live around these parts?" he asked from his seat two stools away from the women.

Filter cigarettes answered, "Yeah darl'n, just up the block a bit. You look'n for a little company and excitement before you go home?"

"No, but thanks for asking, I'll just stay married and faithful for the time being," he said. Collin offered his name once their drinks arrived. "To the yuletide season, ladies. My name is Paul. Nice to make your acquaintances."

Filtered cigarette said "I'm Pattie. Thanks for the drink. Any time you're in the area, stop by and I'll drink to your health."

"Hi," the second woman replied, "I'm Grace and I'm just visiting my boyfriend for the week. He'll be by any minute now, I hope. The bastard is always late, like a fuck'n prima-donna. He thinks he's Sir Lancelot, for God sake." A gust of cold air suddenly rushed into the bar as a lanky fellow entered, stamping his feet to shake off imaginary snow. He made a beeline for Grace and seeing that Collin was chatting with his girl, he sat between them.

"Sorry I'm late baby. The damn truck wouldn't start. I had to push it out into the street and coast downhill to get it going. I'll need a new battery before Christmas," he said. The tattooed barmaid delivered a hot rum drink to the fellow without his asking. He was obviously a regular. Pattie seemed to know him but didn't let on. You do that for customers when they are with their women. Collin sensed their connection and the electricity their odd glances created between them.

Collin moved past the new arrival and sat next to Pattie who was just stubbing out her cigarette. "I'm going over to the Mud Puddle Tavern for a nightcap," Pattie said, "care to join me?" She too was fishing.

"No thanks, not tonight. I need my sleep. It is a long drive home to Philly in the morning," Collin said. The woman downed her drink and rose on her unsteady, overly exposed legs. "Suit yourself, darl'n. See you around next year, maybe." She sashayed to the door like a party girl, advertising her happy mood.

Collin took a small notepad from his pocket, wrote a brief description of Pattie and made note of the bar's name. Unobserved, he extracted the last filtered cigarette butt from the ashtray that she had smoked.

He would develop her DNA profile from the saliva on the cigarette butt. Pattie would be his first fish of many he planned to catch as organ donors. He turned his attention to the drunk father in the booth across from him. The pair were still arguing and from what he overheard, the father lived nearby with the boy's mother. She had invited the son for dinner and had asked him to fetch his father home from the bar as dinner was about to be served. The father was intent on consuming as much booze as humanly possible before that happened.

"You sound just like your damn mother, Donnie. God help me but you truly do. Stop your constant nagging and we will skedaddle out of here after I have one for the ditch," his father scolded, and he signaled the barmaid.

"OK Pop, but just one and that's it. Then we're finished, right?" Donnie Jr. asked.

"Yes boy, if you say so," Donnie Sr. said and his shifty eyes darted about the bar, seeking one of his drinking pals. He needed to be rescued. He hated to go home so early, without a good glow-on from a belly full of the Dutchman's cheap whiskey. It was payday and he was still flush.

When the father and son finally left, Collin scooped the father's shot-glass from their table as he went to the men's toilet. He put it in a small paper bag, along with the other DNA sample, and then put them both into his inside coat pocket. In only one hour he had lined-up two potential donors. He left the bar and proceeded to his car in the parking lot next door.

He placed the two samples into a legal-sized envelope and removed his pea-coat. Disguised in a courier's jacket now, he dropped them through the night delivery-box at Sid Fournier's attorney office.

Sid occasionally needed DNA tests to prove relationship status in some of his estate cases. When a long-lost relative showed up to claim a large estate, he was naturally suspicious. To confirm their identity, he had a local government lab facility do work-ups on covertly collected DNA samples. They were under-the-table, no-questions-asked, cash transactions. If the claimant turned out to be a fraud, he would petition the courts for a legal DNA test. It was part of his service to the few wealthy clients he had.

Collin had advised Sid that until he had his own lab running, he would need to identify blood and DNA samples to ensure live-donor recipients got a healthy organ. What he didn't explain, was that DNA samples normally came via a swab of the inner mouth of the donor. Sid didn't ask and Collin didn't volunteer information as to how these samples were obtained. The lawyer used the same method to collect samples and just never gave the situation a second thought.

Collin used the DNA test to determine the tissue or leukocyte antigen (HLA) type, blood-type and race of his potential donors. With this information, he would be able to match organs to those waiting on the nationwide recipient donor list. He was uncomfortable using traditional test-labs as it exposed his operation to outside scrutiny. Soon, he would have his own private and secure DNA extraction laboratory at home.

Since his return to work after the accident, Collin had nearly worked himself to death. Between his 12-hour shifts at the hospital and an average of four hours spent setting up his clinic at home, he was exhausted. The chief surgeon, Dr. Luis Palmer, a kind, elderly gentleman called Collin into his office for a private talk.

"It has been a great relief to all of us here at Mass. Hospital, to have you back at work," he said. "I'm concerned that you will burn yourself out at the pace you've set for yourself. Therefore, you will need to cut back on your operating hours significantly. Until further notice, your operating duties will be reduced to four hours every other day. Now, there will be no argument from you. This is non-negotiable."

It was a shock, to hear Dr. Palmer's pronouncement. He had been happy to be back at work these past two months. It was the first time that he had slept peacefully since his family's death. He fell asleep exhausted each night and rarely had his disturbing nightmares. He was so pre-occupied with his work that it left no room for the pain of death to creep into his psyche. He realized he may have been using exhaustion to medicate and alleviate his pain. He was so focused on his plans that he lost sight of the looming mental abyss he could collapse into. He decided to take a week off work and return to a less demanding schedule as the chief surgeon had suggested.

"Thank you, doctor. I didn't notice what I was getting myself into. Yes, I have been using exhaustion as a sleep-aid and now I see the fallacy of that. I'll take a week or two of my vacation time, if that's OK with you. When I return, I will adapt to a lighter schedule, as you suggest," Collin said.

For the next two weeks Collin built a pottery wheel and a kiln in the children's basement play area. It would be his new hobby, a ruse to fool the neighbors. The few clay and ceramic bowls and figurines he produced would be given as gifts to neighbors. It would be the perfect cover for his many absences, while working in his basement clinic or using the crematorium.

The electric oven had an operating temperature range of 1,500 to 2,500 ^{0}F. The lower temperatures would bisque the clay for decorating and the higher temperatures would set the ceramic finishes. As for human body cremation, that called for a mid-temperature setting of 1,800 degrees for 2 to 3 hours. The exhaust was fed through a vapor-scrubber before being fed up the chimney of the ground-floor fireplace.

Making pottery is not a one-day process. It requires weeks to perfect. Many hours of firing are needed to develop the raw clay objects into various stages of the finished product. It was too time consuming for Collin to make pottery and still run his organ clinic. He purchased the figurines and bowls, telling everyone that he made them. Collin's neighbors were pleased that he had found a hobby to take his mind off his loss and he was happy to have devised a perfect cover for his covert clinic.

Every few nights Collin would head out in his car to a poorer district, of which there were several, in and around Boston. He was acquiring quite a lengthy list of potential organ donors. Being able to do the DNA workups in his own lab was a great stress-relief for Collin. Sid Fournier and his Lab Tech no longer had a clue as to how many donors were available. When a specific blood-type, heart or other organ was required, he had no trouble finding the perfect match with one of the fish on his list.

The cremation process was not capable of rendering a body to ashes completely. Parts of some large bones, pacemakers and teeth remained, as well as dental fillings and metal bone splints. The metal pieces were disposed of in his hospital's recycle bins. The other fragments were ground to a powder in a small cone-crusher. He told his neighbors that the adjustable cone crusher was to render his mistakes into re-useable clay powder. This usually got a nervous laugh from the women and a smile of understanding from the men. None of his neighbors wanted to upset the doctor due to his perceived fragile state.

Dr. MacDonald had a large empty bag labeled Nitric Garden Ash to store the cremated cadaver ashes. He dug it into the soil of his red cedar shade trees and flowering southern magnolias that grew close to the house. He also used it sparingly in the flower gardens to increase the soil's ph. balance.

When Collin puttered about in his front garden, the neighbors would smile their pretentious, tolerant smiles and leave him to his chores. They tended to walk on eggshells around the poor doctor, fearing they might somehow drive him back into his deep despair. All Collin did was to get rid of the ashes from the crematorium.

Chapter 3

ORGAN DELIVERIES

Collin pulled into the MacDonald's Restaurant parking lot off #9 Highway in Brookline to transfer his organs to Sid Fournier's SUV. The two small ice coolers were in the trunk, filled with their precious cargo. The ploy was to park in a blind spot of the security camera while Sid went into the fast-food joint for a snack. Meanwhile, Collin quickly transferred the coolers into the back of Sid's SUV. It was simple and efficient. Sid had the appropriate paperwork identifying that the skin grafts came from a New York City middle-aged female suicide. The two kidneys came from a motorcycle-accident victim in New Hampshire. Everything appeared neat and as it should be. Collin and Sid had learned that people were overjoyed to get the needed organs. Other than ensuring that they were fresh, of the right size, leukocyte antigen (HLA) type and blood type, very few questions were asked. The fact that they were delivered by a National Organ Donor Registry (NODR) courier, enhanced the legitimacy of the process.

This evening, Sid had arrived first and Collin pulled into the lot beside his empty vehicle. Just as he put the coolers in the back, all hell broke loose. Alarms went off, and the distant emergency vehicle sirens grew louder. People poured out of the two exit doors screaming hysterically.

"Run! Run! He has a knife. Look out! Someone help me, I can't find my child!" There were a multitude of shouts that Collin couldn't discern, coming from the chaos. Sid surfaced in the scrambling crowd, dodging toddlers and seniors as he leapt past the less fit, to save himself. When he got to his SUV, he recognized Collin and almost blew his cover.

"What's happening?" Collin shouted at him to give Sid time to collect his wits.

"Some nutcase is robbing the place and he has a butcher knife. He's swinging it at everyone. Several people are hurt and bleeding. Oh God, it's a mess in there," he said as he fumbled for his cellphone to call 911.

"Don't do that! I can hear the emergency vehicles coming. Get in your car and leave via the back exit to return to Boston. I'll attend to the injured and call you on a cell burner-phone in about an hour," Collin said. He had his back turned away from Sid, pretending that they were strangers to the security cameras and the fleeing people.

Realty quickly kicked-in for the lawyer. He was in his SUV even before Collin had finished speaking. Without a look or a nod of recognition, Sid drove slowly out of the parking area, heading for #9 Highway East. Collin got his travel medical bag from the trunk and jogged to the restaurant door. The police had tasered the robber, a young Hispanic kid, high on drugs and wanting money to buy more.

Collin introduced himself as a surgeon and the lead investigator directed him to the far wall, where the injured were assembled. A group of adults and children suffered from defensive cut-wounds to their arms and hands. His triage review directed him to a young Irish boy with a major slash cut across his face and a knife puncture wound to his stomach. He was the worst of the lot, Collin surmised after a quick examination. He placed a clean compression pad against the boy's stomach and told him to press it into his abdomen. He then attended to the major facial cut. This fellow had been first in line at the counter when the robber came in. On instinct, he had reacted defensively, and he would have to live with the scars of his injuries to remind him of that mistake.

Collin cleaned the flap of skin and tissue, pressed it closed with his gloved hand, then started to wrap a gauze bandage around the head to hold a surgical pad tightly over the wound. It would temporarily stop the facial bleeding. *Head wounds always bled profusely*, he thought to himself. He could now return to attend to the stomach puncture which was far more serious. A cut and bleeding internal organ required immediate surgery. As he bent over the boy, two EMD's entered the complex. The Police Sargent pointed them in Collin's direction and advised them that he was a doctor.

It always amazed Collin and others in his profession that no one ever asked for identification at times like this. It was accepted that he was who he said he was, a surgeon. The two private company medics were the first to arrive and Collin instructed one of them to call for back-up. They needed an air ambulance with a physician on the flight crew pronto. It was imperative to get the Irish boy into surgery as quickly as possible. The EMS next to Collin passed the request onto one of the police officers, while the other one shook his head in disagreement.

"Delay that call officer. It's a gut wound for sure and bleeding internally. We can get him to New England Surgicare Hospital faster than an aerial unit. It's only two miles north of here. I'm an ex-army medic, I've seen lots of wounds like this. We'll take care of him now," he said. In a take-charge manner that reassured Collin, the medic installed an IV into the patient and the other began recording his vitals.

More ambulances arrived. The boy was on his way to surgery in under two minutes and Collin knew he would make it now. The rest of the injured in the room were attended to and now the officer in charge came to speak with Collin. The first question that came out of the investigating sergeant's mouth, set the tone of the interview.

"What brings you to MacDonald's on a winter's evening," he asked. "Seems a little odd for a surgeon to be eating at a fast food place like this."

"Since I lost my family to a DUI driver awhile back, I just don't feel like cooking after a long surgical shift," Collin replied.

"What's your name and address sir," came the next question.

After providing the information, recognition came into the Sergeants eyes as he recalled Collin surname.

"Yes, now I remember, Collin and Tracy MacDonald, the doctor and their three kids. God man, I attended that scene. I am so sorry for your loss. Here, sit down in this booth with me until I finish my report on your involvement, then you are free to go," the Sargent said. The police officer's suspicious demeanor had morphed into one that was more friendly, which was reflected in his manner of questioning.

"Thank you, Doctor, for your help here tonight," the sergeant said. "Should you ever need assistance from the police, here is my card. I would be honored to be of service to you," Sargent Warner Brierley said.

True to the Sargent's word, Collin was on his way within five minutes. The robbery established his presence at the restaurant that February evening. That had the potential to expose Sid Fournier's presence, if the police confiscated the security tapes of the back-parking lot. It was a chance he took in this line of business. He and Sid would need to set up a new venue to exchange information and organs.

They discussed the possibility of using a bus terminal storage-locker for the exchange. It was just a matter of having an extra key cut. The problem was, keyless lockers that ran out of allotted storage time were opened and re-keyed. They found a solution by joining a tennis club where they could use the locker system in the members' shower to make their exchanges.

The Tennis and Racquet Club on Boylston Street suited their needs well. They were open from 10 a.m. to 11 p.m. weeknights and closed 3 hours earlier on weekends. The large and diversified membership allowed them to blend in easily, with little chance of exposing their association. The men's locker-room had panels of lockers in several rooms, affording them enough privacy to store a cooler inside an inconspicuous duffle bag. They were back in business.

Chapter 4

THE FISHING TRIP

Later, in March, Sid called on a burner cell to inform Collin he urgently needed a heart for a type B-, 52-year old white woman, weighing 110 lbs. She was on a heart machine in a Boston Hospital and was not expected to live more than a week. This was the type of urgent request that Sid hated to burden Collin with. He assumed that Collin would call his medical friends and look under every rock to find a matching donor. It might be someone who had suffered a brain death injury. He didn't know and he was even less anxious to learn.

It was a simple task for Collin, but he was not about to explain that to his partner. Under the heading "shopping lists" on his lab computer, he sourced type O- & type B- female blood types. The resulting short list contained nine female candidates, obtained through his fishing expeditions, who all matched his search criteria. Next, he added the 110 lbs. to his spreadsheet search, and this narrowed down the list to just two results.

One was Pattie, the drunk hooker he had met at the Dutchman's Bar in Boston. The other was a multiple DUI offender, named Hazel, from Framingham, further east, off the turnpike. He selected Pattie and decided to visit the Mud Puddle Tavern to find her, rather than returning to the Dutchman's for the second time in four months.

Dressed in his dockworker outfit again, he headed over to the Eastie of Boston and parked next door to the Mud Puddle. It was about 8:00 p.m. He recalled that the last time he had seen Pattie, she was just leaving the Dutchmen's to go to the Mud Puddle for a nightcap. That meant she probably worked the streets and bars in the afternoons and early evenings when there was less violence. *Smart girl. You can never be too cautious these days,* he thought. Collin's luck held and Pattie was at the bar chatting with a female customer.

In December when he was still new at this business of collecting donors, he felt he had to set up elaborate scenarios to cover a person's disappearance. He recalled a guy who was about to do a stretch in the state prison for his third DUI. After lacing his drink with GHB, Collin had maneuvered him into the back of his Lexus with great difficulty due to the heavy topcoat the man wore. He set that one up as a bridge-jumper into the Charles River. There was never any mention of the suicide in the paper. In fact, none of his victims had ever been reported as missing in the newspapers. These were apparently expendable people. So, he just collected them now. They went straight to the clinic, without the elaborate cover of a disappearing act.

"Hi stranger, your name is Paul, isn't it? You have family up in Philly somewhere?" Pattie asked.

"Right on all counts. You have an excellent memory," Collin said and switched to using his alias, Paul.

"Yes. Well, when we last met you were too shy to accompany a lady to her home for a little comfort and fun," she said with a giggle.

"If the invitation is still open, I would be happy to escort you this evening," he said.

"Well that will definitely brighten my evening darl'n," she purred. "Buy me a Whiskey Sour, while I go powder my nose," she said.

She felt almost giddy. It had been slow night so far with just those two college kids wanting a blowjob in their van. Not much money tonight, she thought but that was about to change.

"Sounds like a plan, you live over on Arlington Street, don't you?" Paul asked, "I have my car in the lot next door, we can drive if that is OK with you."

"Sure honey, anything you want, I'll be right back. Don't start without me," and she giggled again.

When the bartender delivered the drink for Pattie and a bottle of Bud for Collin, he didn't look twice at Collin. He only saw another jerk who had to buy his sex from a hooker. Scum, he thought and returned to wiping glasses.

Collin poured a small dose of GHB into Pattie's drink, satisfied that it wasn't obvious or cloudy. The slight salty taste would be covered by the flavor of the Whiskey Sour. She returned from the Ladies Room with a smile a mile wide and a bounce in her step that could pass for a model's catwalk strut. She downed her drink almost too quickly for Collin's purpose. The date-rape drug would still take another ten minutes to kick in for this small woman.

In the car, she slid across to Collin and put her hand on his crotch. This was Pattie's safety check, to see if he was a cop. Cop's hate being touched that way and she wanted her date thinking about having sex with her.

"Oh honey, we are going to have a good time tonight, you will just love the way I've decorated my place. I've got music and mirrors and candles. All the good stuff and a little blow if you're into that," she said.

Her speech began to slur and trail off. Her head fell slowly onto Collin's shoulder as he drove the car down Arlington Street. Turning the heat up, he set the radio to a soft love song. Pattie would become oblivious to the world within two minutes. This part of the fishing trip was going as planned.

Getting from downtown Boston in the early evening with every cop on the road patrolling for drunken drivers, was not easy. He didn't want to risk being stopped with this hooker in his car. That would be a game changer if he was stopped for some reason. He would have to dump her and go out to Framingham to pick up Hazel.

Minding the speed limit and staying just a little back of the car in front, he looked the same as most commuters on the road that evening. He was heading home on autopilot with the little lady asleep on his shoulder. *Lucky bastard*, the cops thought. *They still had a full shift to work.*

He pulled into his driveway, opened the garage door with his fob's signal and entered quickly. Getting inside safely, without the neighbors noticing his passenger, was half the battle. It would be a disaster if one of them came to see who the new woman in his life was. He lifted her small frame onto the collapsible gurney with ease. He put his dockworker jacket and toque in the trunk. With the woman now strapped onto the rolling table, he headed for the elevator entrance to the clinic, through the garage inside, house door.

Opening the hallway coat-closet, he slid the few coats to one side and activated the hidden switch near the ceiling. The back wall moved to one side and the elevator invited them in. Once in the clinic, he put on his fresh whites, skull cap, face mask and gloves. The removal of the patient's clothing was facilitated by the styles she chose to wear. Clothing that could quickly be removed was part of her trade. Putting a backless hospital gown on her, finished this phase of the procedure.

She would be out until at least midnight, so Collin had his work cut out for himself. She had to be prepared for major surgery and the condition of her health was yet to be determined. He was pleased with what he saw up to this point. The lab tests would confirm his hopes for a good candidate for the heart transplant.

The first step was to collect urine and blood samples on a regular basis. For that he installed an IV in the small artery on the back of her right hand and an IV stint into a vein on the inside of her arm. He hooked up an IV drip to the stint. Next, he installed a catheter for urine collection and a diaper for solid waste. The final intrusion was a nasal drip feeding-tube, inserted into her nostril. He covered that with a plastic oxygen mask. He attached a heart-monitor that emitted a reassuring beep with every beat of her heart. It beeped a slow, at rest 77 beats per minute.

Collin then strapped the girl firmly to the operating table using wrist, arm, leg and body straps. He covered her with a warm blanket and began his first test work on the blood he had collected. It indicated she was lacking in several essential vitamins, C, D, most of the B series and Iron. With this information, he injected those vitamins in extracted liquid form into the Y-receiver on the IV drip. He would wait to collect enough urine to test the base discharge amounts. Then he could monitor the body's ability to metabolize the doses he had administered.

It was shaping up to be a busy night as he prepared a second blood test to confirm the health of her vital organs. The urine samples would be used to test her kidney function.

Pattie would wake up soon. He prepared the clinic for that eventuality. He could not keep her drugged and also maintain good organ condition. He had to clear up any nutritional deficiencies and infections such as STD's if they were present. Her mental attitude was important to absorbing and metabolizing the vitamins and nutrients he had injected.

He turned on the background elevator music he had on the CD player and dimmed the lights in the operating area. He then pulled the curtain to ¾ of the way around the bed. With the heart and oxygen monitors flashing their digital information, the ICU scene was established. He got his clear plastic operating gown on and sealed it with tape to appear as protection from airborne infection.

When Pattie came out of the GHB drug's grasp, her heartrate increased rapidly. Collin pretended to be a very attentive nurse technician in a specialized isolation ward at the university hospital. Only his eyes were visible behind the face-shield. He looked every bit the part he was playing. It only had to work for a day, perhaps two at the longest.

"Pattie, Pattie, can you hear me? You're OK now, we have you secure in the University Hospital. Pattie, are you with me? Blink your eyes to let me know," Collin said. He was now posing as Dr. Peter McKinney, an intern, complete with name tag. While the fake hospital setting may have seemed like overkill, Collin felt obligated to provide good clean transplant organs. That goal was of utmost importance and the small amount of effort required to deceive the donor until he removed their organs seemed negligible to him.

Pattie was more lucid now and she was concerned. The last thing she remembered was sitting in the Mud Puddle hoping for a nice customer for a change. That one college boy had a strange odor about him, and it was not the usual smell of pot.

"Where am I, did I... did I get in an accident?" she asked.

"No, you are quite fine now. You gave us a bit of a scare earlier, but you are a trooper. You are pulling through just fine. Try to relax so the anti-bacterial drugs can do their work," the intern said. "Can you wiggle your toes for me?" he asked. When she responded, he asked her to squeeze his fingers with her hand. "Good. Yes, that is very good, indeed," he said. "Your motor skills are slowly returning."

She was coming out of the rape drug's control, so Collin administered a light sedative to the IV supply. He made bogus notes on the clip board by her bed and when she spoke it was the question he had planned for.

"What the hell is going on?" Pattie asked. She was now almost fully awake and speaking with a street drawl. Her eyes darted to the various monitors and instruments around her bed. She had tried to move but the restraints held her firmly. "Why am I strapped down? What the hell is going on here?" she demanded.

"You were found unconscious in the parking lot next to the Mud Puddle Tavern, by a bar patron. The ambulance attendant recognized the symptoms of your medical issue and brought you to the University for the antibodies to treat your infection. It is a fast-acting bacterial lung infection you picked up."

"How did I get infected with that?" she asked. She started to believe what she was being told and she was frightened. *Am I going to die*? she wondered.

"We traced the source to a college student, found unconscious at the Dutchman's Bar two blocks away," the intern said. "It is a highly infectious airborne organism. You are in our very new and modern, isolation ward at the University. You are in very good hands here, so try to relax and allow the drugs to do their job. Alright young lady?"

"Am I going to be alright? Will I get better? How long have I been here?" The questions came in rapid succession as she was now fully awake.

"Why can't I move? Am I paralyzed? God no, not that," she said and began to cry softly.

"You are restrained for your own protection from the seizures you had. Any movement on your part will slow the anti-bacteria drugs from doing their job," he lied. "You have been in our care for two days now," he lied again. "You must lay still and be quiet for the drugs to do their job. You are getting better now that the antibacterial drugs have taken effect. Be a good girl for me, Pattie and try to sleep. Would you like a sleeping pill, would that help?" he asked.

"Yes please," was all she said. Fifteen minutes later she was sound asleep. The heart monitor issued its steady beeps at 72 per minute and falling as she went deeper into REM sleep.

Collin continued the blood and urine tests until he saw that she was metabolizing the vitamins, while the feeding tube fed her nutrients. With the IV keeping her hydrated, he saw no need for further surveillance of her. He would catch a few hours of rest before checking her vitals again in the morning.

She should sleep for about six hours, he thought, as he went up the elevator to the main floor of his home. He would get a few hours' sleep and set his alarm clock for 7:00 am.

She was awake when he returned the next morning. "Did you rest well, Pattie," he asked, maintaining his good bedside manner.

"What time is it and how long have I been here, did you say?" she asked.

"The clock on the wall says it 7:12 a.m. Oh, the curtain is covering the clock. Here I'll open them a little more," he said. "You have been here for a while. This is your third day and it looks as if you could leave by tomorrow afternoon or the next day. That is, if your blood test is clear and you behave and don't move around too much," he lied to her.

"My nose is itchy, and I can't scratch it, could you let me have one hand loose, I promise I'll only move it occasionally. Please," she begged.

The security straps were buckled below the table, out of her reach and Collin saw no reason her left-hand strap couldn't be removed as he had the IV in her right arm and hand. "OK, I will remove the strap holding your left hand, but keep in mind you are under constant observation on a TV monitors at the nurse's station. I will be very upset if they report that you have been moving too much," he said.

"When is breakfast? I could eat a horse," she said in reply.

"You are having it. That is what the tube in your nose is for and that maybe the cause of the itching. We have been feeding you delicious meals these past three days. If you need a diaper changed, you just let me know.

"A bed pan requires too much movement for your lungs to handle. You would pass out if you raised your head even a few inches," he lied. He had her secured so she wouldn't escape. His requirement for her to remain still for medical reasons was an excuse to secure her.

"I do shut off the TV connection to the nurse's station when I changed your diaper. Is that OK?" he said.

Fortunately, Pattie was not very savvy in the ways of the medical world. She had street smarts but those were of no use in this situation. She resigned herself to behave and do as the nice intern requested. It never occurred to her that only one person had attended her during the presumed four-day period. When her vital signs indicated that all was well with her organs, Collin proceeded to the next phase of her captivity. She stopped being just a fish. She had now become an organ donor.

Collin called his partner to arrange a time to transfer the organs that afternoon and then got dressed to perform the operation.

He set the timer for two hours. This would turn on the pottery kiln so it would automatically ramp up to the required 1,800 degrees Fahrenheit needed for cremation. It would take an hour. Meanwhile, he would begin to remove the needed organs.

The stronger sedative put her into a gentle, deep sleep. Collin prepared her body for the major surgery. She would donate her heart, which was her prime reason for her being there. She also would donate a lung, her liver, kidneys and pancreas with a section of intestine. Lastly, both her eyes, complete with corneas would be used for medical training at the eye bank.

He began the three-hour operation. Working alone was a major issue that required timing and planning. Not all organs can survive for the same length of time without a blood source. This period can be extended by immersing them in nutritional preserving fluids, then packing the organs in ice once they are removed.

He harvested the organs as quickly as he could, taking care to ensure the transplant surgeon had sufficient material to do their job. To provide a good product, he took great care in the removal process. It was paramount to ensure his standard of service was always met. The still beating heart and lungs were the last organs removed. This allowed a steady supply of blood around the body while he worked.

He labelled each cooler-chest, identifying the type of organ, time of harvesting, preservative formula, donor age and time of death. He included the bogus cause of death, as well as the fictitious hospital name, address and the required NODR code number assigned to the patient. When he was done, he placed them on a dolly to be transported to his car.

The body, now in sections was placed in a four-by three-foot cremation tray along with his operating clothes, which he slid into the preheated kiln. He threw the switch to start the exhaust scrubber and set the shutdown time for three hours. This part of the procedure was complete.

He had time for a light lunch and then headed to his meeting at the Tennis Club. Pattie had been in his home a total of 15-hours. As Collin pulled out onto his driveway, Steve, his next-door neighbor called to him and he rolled down his window to chat.

"Hi Doc. Where are you off to today?" Steve asked. He had a grass rake in one hand and wiped his brow with the other. He was cutting his grass for the first time that spring and it was tough going.

"I'm going to speak with your gardener to see if he can do my lawn when he does yours next time. If you see him, will you let him know I am interested?" Steve asked.

"Sure, I can do that for you, Steve. How's the wife and kids?" he asked, being polite. He really didn't like either of them. They were nosy and pushy.

"They're all fine. Kids are dreaming of summer vacation, same old thing. You know how it is," he said.

It was too late. He had mentioned the children and feared setting Collin off on a downhill slope into depression once again. Seeing all the coolers in the back seat, Steve tried to change the subject.

"You're going to the river for more of that clay you like to make pottery out of, aren't you? Well enjoy your afternoon. It's supposed to be nice all day," he said. Turning quickly to end the conversation, he headed for his own yard. Seeing the wisp of vapor coming from Collin's chimney he said, "I see you're still working hard on your ceramics, good for you Collin." It came out condescending and he kicked himself again. *Damn, it was hard talking to the guy since his family had been killed.*

"Have a nice day, Steve. Say hello to the wife and it is bisquing I'm doing today, I'll fire next week," he said and drove off.

In his mind, Collin had finally resolved his issues with the loss of his family. This new adventure into clandestine organ supply had done that. The neighbors were still walking on eggshells as far as his mental state was concerned and that suited him just fine. It kept the nosy neighbors at bay.

Sid would not meet him today. He would time his arrival once Collin was clear of the tennis facility. He would drop off more donor labels for Collin with the transaction documents for the last four offshore money transfers. Collin, for his part, would leave the five small coolers stuffed in a gym bag. These he would put in Sid's locker, to be rerouted into the national organ donor supply line.

Just how Sid handled his end of the routing was as mysterious to Collin as the organ collection process was to Sid. The less a person knew, the better the security of the operation was. Sid and Collin knew that and always had a backup scenario for every phase of their venture, in the event it was compromised.

Chapter 5

LIEUTENANT FARNSWORTH BPD

It was the fiftieth Missing Person Report, (MPR) he had received in his area of Eastie in the past six months. Usually the down and out in his precinct just overdosed or did the plastic bag trip and their body turned up when the rent wasn't paid. Pattie Dumfries was the second MPR this May, and the month was not over yet.

If a skidrow person wants to disappear, there are half a dozen seedy areas around Boston where they can go. He knew them all. Mattapan and Roxbury were just as bad as his own precinct, so he would look there first. He called his counterparts in both areas, provided a description and missing person's file, MPF number. With that information, his counterparts could see the complete data file on their own computers.

He checked out the last known address provided by the person filing the MPR. His first impression upon seeing Pattie's flat was to conclude that she was a hooker. This assumption was based on the room's décor, and it was blatantly obvious to him. Unless, of course, she was totally into herself. He asked around the neighborhood about the girl and her habits. This information had not been forthcoming and there may have been a dozen reasons for that. The main one being that the person filing the report didn't want to discredit the character of the missing person. When he had exhausted all the standard search procedures, he returned to his office.

Lieutenant Cody Farnsworth was a 16-year veteran of the Boston Police Department. He was of British descent and at age 40, he still had a full head of red hair, which he hated with a passion. Another thing he hated was missing children, particularly in his precinct. Molestation and child abuse were escalating in this area of town. His transfer two-years earlier from the Bunco Squad where he investigated fraud, gambling and con-games, to the Missing Person's (MPs) Department. Transferring had been a salvation for Cody.   He preferred the variety. His new MP cases generally dealt with missing husbands and boyfriends. The lowlife characters he had to deal with while he had served on the Bunco Squad had been deflating.

Most MP cases followed a clean and predictable pattern. If they didn't want to be found, he would respect that. He would inform the friend or relative that the person was well and healthy. He told them that they were in a happy phase of their life and when they felt the need, they would contact the seeker. He would file a similar report at the department with the MPs address and a request for confidentiality. Case closed.

What information he had managed to collect from these recent cases was not much, but his stomach told him something was out of place. Like the last five cases, this one didn't look like a runner. She had no major enemies, was not a junky but she drank too much and had two DUI's to show for it. Her car had been repossessed and other than that, she was clean. No outstanding warrants. Missing your AA meetings was not a felony.

He checked with his peers in the other four poorer neighborhoods of town and got no further in his investigation.

His Captain hated him using the more colorful description of skidrow. *What the hell*, he thought, *it is what it is. Unless you planned to clean up the problems there, why not call it what it was, skidrow.*

At 6'–4", the Lieutenant presented a daunting figure in his police uniform and when he wore his civilian dress suits. He was a senior veteran of the Boston Police Department. He had worked in most precincts around town and had been physically scarred by the experience. He had a knife scar on his cheek and a second belly button from a bullet. His front tooth had a chipped corner from a street fight. He didn't get the chipped tooth fixed because it scared the street punks when he smiled.

A trained eye would notice the swollen knuckles from bare fistfights. His body stance, whenever he felt threatened was a dead giveaway of his ability and disposition. He didn't enjoy his previous three-year stint with the Fraud Squad. Even the year spent as a sergeant in the city jail, on night shift, had been better than Fraud.

He had taken to studying at the University the year he worked at the jail. He found courses on social behavior and psychology that were precursors to a law degree course. His completion of the two courses got him promoted to Staff Sargent and transferred to the

Bunco Squad. He had to continue his studies on the internet due to the grueling hours that fraud investigation demanded. Cody passed with honors and successfully wrote his exams for Lieutenant shortly after.

The fact that he had soft hazel eyes went unnoticed by most people. They only saw his mop of red hair, the broken nose and the chipped tooth.

The other four low-income areas of Boston reported an increase of runners, people who just dropped off the radar screen. They were a mix of social misfits but predominantly drunks.

The drug users ran because they owed money to their suppliers. They usually turned up dead or badly beaten. As for the drunks and their hopes of a fresh start, those were just pipe dreams. Nevertheless, Cody silently wished them well.

The drunks tended to remain in one place, close to a liquor supply where they could drink without too much effort. They tended to run to escape a few months back rent and irate landlords.

He removed drug addicts from his list and narrowed it down to twenty-five people from the four districts. From these, he noticed all had a similar profile. They were drinkers with multiple DUI convictions. They were all between the ages of 25 and 45. These facts got his gut churning. He sensed an old feeling of uneasiness flood through his veins that made him shiver.

The numbers were abnormal. In the four skidrow districts there would usually be a total of 20 missing. Now there were 50 missing, with a similar profile in a six-month period. He checked at the state of Massachusetts statistics for its total number of MPs for the same period. He cataloged them into groups by age, addictions, suspected suicides, debtors, lovers and wanna-be missing spouses.

It was a rough, unprofessional division of groups but it helped him to see the big picture. He searched for a pattern of events across the state, versus what was transpiring in the skidrows of Boston. His university and internet college degrees were being put to good use.

In his prime target of alcoholics with DUI records, the numbers were staggering. Instead of 10 percent of those missing, this group totaled a full 50%. He needed to investigate further, before informing his boss about the anomaly he had uncovered. There was nothing worse than getting your head chopped off because you didn't do your homework, before you spoke to your boss.

Cody sent out inquiries to the four states bordering Massachusetts for the number of MPs with alcoholic and DUI profiles. He wanted to know whether their numbers had increased in the past six months. It was a longshot and time-consuming for dozens of clerks around the northeast. How else could he acquire a handle on a specific type of missing person profile in such a large area?

The Lieutenant knew there would be a certain amount of bitching from cash-strapped states and districts. Even Massachusetts officials were protesting the extra workload. This DUI conviction status was not a category or profile kept by census-keepers. It required someone to extrapolate the numbers from each town and district.

The roof of Cody's world collapsed on the following Monday. He had just returned from assisting with a burglary call when the light on his phone indicated a message. Hoping for new information on one of his cases, he quickly retrieved his messages. There was only one, the Captain's secretary, calling to request the Lieutenant's presence in the Captain's office ASAP. This was not going to be a pat-on-the-back, well-done sort of gathering. Cody's gut was gnawing a hole through his stomach. *Not good*, he thought. *Had he overstepped his authority somehow and didn't know it?*

Whenever he had been called up on the carpet by the Captain before, he was left to cool his heels in the outer office for half an hour at the most. Today he waited 55 minutes before being ushered in. There weren't any magazines to look busy with, while other people filed through the office. Despite his size, the Lieutenant felt small and vulnerable. It was difficult to get comfortable in the wooden chairs the Captain provided for his guests to sit on.

The second Cody entered the office, his Chief of Police took charge. There were three people, not including himself, in his office. The Deputy Superintendent, second in command of the Bureau and the mayor's bootlicking assistant. Both sat at opposite ends of the Captain's desk. The mayor's assistant was known as The Weasel by the Eastie precinct's lower ranks. The Deputy Superintendent had been the Eastie precinct's Captain one year earlier. He got up after Cody sat down. He now stood by the window, no longer in charge. This used to be his office and he didn't like being out of the loop or distanced from the cops on the street.

"Lieutenant, good of you to drop by," his Captain said. "We have an issue to deal with and you are just the fellow that we want to speak to about it." There were nods all around except from Cody. If this was a trap, he was wary and if they needed his help, why did he have to wait outside for 55-minutes?

The mayor's weasel spoke up, interrupting the Captain. "Yes, we're here to learn why you are running up the budget of most of the Atlantic northeast without so much as a how-do-you-do to my office," he sputtered.

"George, I asked you to keep quiet and allow me to conduct this interview. This is my office and I will do the talking in this meeting." Turning back to the Lieutenant he continued, "now Cody, we seem to be at a roadblock here. I gave you the missing persons file for our precinct because you have a good eye for oddities. Your performance has proven that I know my people and the department." *It's always a good idea to show your capability whenever the brass is around,* Cody thought. He didn't smile but he wanted to.

"However, this has created a problem, in that you are disturbing the other four districts and on top of that, going to four state governments for their records," the Captain said. "Your sphere of communication includes the people on the street of this precinct, your fellow officers and this office. You do not go beyond that. Not to the other districts, not our state and for God sakes, not to other adjoining states!" the Chief commanded.

"You have enough experience to know this and yet you chose to overstep your authority, Cody. Why is that, I ask you?"

Lieutenant Farnsworth was the only person in the room looking at the Captain and therefore he was the only one to see that the Captain was smiling. It was not his Captain who required him to be here today, it was the mayor, which meant it was a political complaint. Cody was sufficiently savvy to know how to respond.

"I'm extremely sorry sir. I was caught up in my investigation and obviously overstepped my authority. I am humbled to be in the presence of those here in your office today and ashamed to be the cause of this assembly. Sir, I will offer my resignation to you. Will that be acceptable?" Cody asked. It was a bullshit offer and his Captain knew it.

Looking first to the mayor's assistant and then to his own boss for consensus, the Captain replied, "No, that would be a bit extreme. However, we do appreciate your sincerity. Don't let this happen again." This translated into, next time you go outside our precinct for information, let me know first so I can fight off the political dogs when they start yapping.

"Thank you, sir. How should we proceed with this case?" he asked.

"You were on the right track here, Lieutenant. We will drop the State of New York from your research and concentrate on the two states to the south, Connecticut and Rhode Island. As for New Hampshire, we could reduce their involvement to the Manchester area and south," he said.

"Thank you, Captain. Will there be anything else before I return to my desk?" Cody asked.

"Yes, there is. George," the Captain looked at the Mayor's assistant. "Is there anything else that we need to discuss on this matter or other topics on the Mayor's mind today?"

"I ... well, no, I mean the Mayor has a lot to discuss. Oh... I see, not at the present time. I'll excuse myself. Please carry on with your work Captain. Deputy Superintendent, it was nice seeing you again, good day gentlemen," he stammered. He totally ignored Lieutenant Farnsworth in his hurry to exit the office.

"I just hated dealing with paid city employees, especially the police," George, the Mayor's assistance mumbled under his breath.

After it was confirmed that George had left the outer waiting area, the Captain asked Cody for an update and his impressions on the missing persons file.

"It looks as if someone has a vendetta for drunks or perhaps drunk drivers. Thinking about it, it may be both. The increase of MPs in the other four precincts almost match our own at 30%. Usually a person with a hate for someone, likes to beat the hell out of them and leaves the evidence for us to find in a ditch somewhere. In these cases, nothing is left; no evidence of foul play, no DNA, just plain zero," Cody said. His frustration showed in the frown on his face and his scars took on a whiter shade of pale.

"I have gone to the FBI datalink searching for other cities across the country who have had this type of increase with negative results. I have used different search criteria and still nothing. Until I determine that this is a local anomaly or more wide-spread, I am unable to come to any logical conclusions," Cody said.

"Thank you, Cody. Well, Deputy Mikael, do you have any eureka thoughts or ideas that will help us resolve this matter?" the Captain asked.

"No, John. Cody has about covered every point and then some. I will put a little pressure on the surrounding districts and out-of-state police departments for their input. Keep me informed, especially when you determine exactly what area of the northeast is being affected. Now I must see the Mayor before George gets everything we discussed screwed up. The Mayor might call in the National Guard. Good day Cody, keep up the good work. John, I'll call you later, after I see the Mayor."

The Deputy Superintendent vacated his place at the window and rushed out of the office. Captain John Evenly, looked at the assistant mayor's vacant seat and considered having it fumigated. Instead, he sat in the chair the Deputy Superintendent was to sit on and looked Cody in the eye.

"Do we have a serial killer on the loose, Cody? Is the reincarnation of the Boston Strangler walking our streets, again?" he asked.

"I don't know, but I plan to find out. Let's not let this get out and cause a panic in the skidrows of town," Cody said. He knew in an instant the boss was pissed off with the term.

"It is low-income, Cody, for God sakes, low-income. Is that so hard to remember?" John said. "Now get back to work and find the perps responsible for this mess."

About the middle of December, a jumper, Jim Fairchild, took a leap off the University Bridge and just missed landing on the railway bridge below. His topcoat was found on top of his shoes at the side of the bridge with his wallet stuffed in the toe of one shoe. He was a three-time convicted DUI and was to be sentenced the following week. It appeared that he took his own life rather than having a judge sentence him to jail time. It was assumed his body had been carried out to sea by the Charles River.

What seemed odd to the detective was the way the coat lay on top of the shoes. Cody had gone over that scenario several times and had even undressed at home to see how he would carry out that procedure. The topcoat always came off before removing the shoes. It didn't make sense to stand on a cold wet sidewalk in your stocking feet, then remove your wallet and topcoat.

It was more likely that the topcoat would come off first and then hung over the railing. The wallet could be put either in a pocket or the shoes, but the shoes would not be placed side by side, as in a store display. They would be removed by using the toe of his foot against the heel of the other shoe, pulling the shoe off. The shoes would be randomly placed on the sidewalk.

He called his Chief to ask for approval to expend some of their budget on forensic work to test the clothing. He wasn't sure what they would find but there might be a hair or skin fragment of an unknown person that didn't fit. With that approval, Cody went down to Evidence Storage and had the items transferred up to the fourth-floor Forensic Department.

A week and a half later he got a report back from the forensic lab detailing their findings. Cocaine was found on the MasterCard and driver's license. Both were stored in a pouch inside the wallet. A random thumb print was found on a coat button that did not belong to the victim. Flecks of wool were found on the coat that may have come from the floor mats of a newer model Lexus car.

There were minute foreign skin fragments in the stretched fabric at the back of the coat. These were found near the collar but were too small for DNA testing. It appeared as if someone had pulled on the coat's collar, stretching the fabric and leaving trace DNA behind.

Cody firstly, ruled out the cocaine. Almost every credit card in America had traces of these drugs, through contact in ATM machines. The stretched wool and thumbprint were well worth the cost of the forensic tests. If this jumper was part of the suspicious MP's group, Cody now had a lead. Seldom did a body float out to sea before being spotted by the people who worked on the Charles River system.

As for the small untestable skin fragments in the stretched fabric on the back of the topcoat, they had him confused. He would have to mull that one over to make sense of it. Cody had a full morning of working the various MP's cases from every angle. He headed to a little greasy spoon called Topper's across from the department for some fresh air and lunch. There, he joined four other detectives who were eating their noon meal.

"Here's the guy who was used to clean Captain Evenly's floor this morning," his friend Paul said.

"God Cody, you were gone for hours, what was the beef?" Louis asked.

"Someone said they saw the mayor's weasel leave the building about 11 a.m. and the Deputy Super soon after," Michaela, the only female at the table, said.

"Cody are you in trouble?" she asked.

"Look people, I was called in to help explain the MP's procedures to the dumbest city employee the chief could find, that is all. It's not a news item, OK? Now drop it and eat your lunch."

The four resumed their topics of discussion; the upcoming baseball season, fishing, kids and spouses. The only two singles at the table were Cody and Michaela, who were single by choice and for no other reason. There are many unwritten codes that bind the of police agency members. Respect for another's privacy was uppermost in those codes.

Chapter 6

GOING FISHING, DOWN SOUTH
IN RHODE ISLAND

After dropping off the gym bag of donor organs at the tennis club, Collin considered doing a little fishing. The fish in the ponds of donors around Boston's skidrows were getting harder and harder to catch. It was a game to him, mental gymnastics to outsmart a drunk. He had expanded his search area to 15-miles around Boston and now he determined it was time to go out of state.

As he drove south aimlessly, he found himself on the #95 highway. He selected Providence, 40 miles away, as his destination. Rhode Island had several large cities and large cities have skidrows.

The hour-long drive gave him time to think about his new life and what he was doing. He reasoned that what he did was not immoral. It was beneficial to people who led a proper life and needed a little luck finding a replacement organ. As Collin saw it, the supply of organs was being disrupted by bureaucratic red tape.

He and Sid had helped over a hundred people these past six months. One hundred people who were alive, loving their families and being loved in return. At what cost? Very little, as he saw it. A few lowlife drunks who were a menace on the roads. They were self-destructive people who would be dead in ten years anyway. Their lifestyles destroyed their organs, making them unusable for transplants. It was better to collect them now, before that happened.

He found his fish to be of reasonable intelligence. They were chatty, with a tendency to brag of their close calls with the Highway Patrol. Within minutes of sitting beside them in a bar, he would extract their life story. With a little prompting and a few drinks, he could decide if they were qualified to be a donor or not. It was preferable that they were single, in reasonable health and fit. He meant fit in the sense that they did not weigh 300 lbs. A body that size took a lot of electricity to cremate. Besides, they were hard to handle by himself.

When the preliminary examination proved that they were of acceptable stock, he needed to collect a DNA sample to find their race and genetic acceptability. This required a certain degree of sleight of hand and at times, even a magical flair. In the past, he had collected toothpicks, used tissues, shot glasses and cigarette butts. If it contained DNA and was left unnoticed, he would slide it into a pocket for later test work.

He used Google maps searches on community computers to find towns and city skidrows for likely bars to fish in. He never used his computer at home for these searches as it was too risky. The way Google captured your URL and promoted products and other site locations based upon your search, irritated him. The fact the computer kept a secondary log of your site visits scared him. It was too traceable, and he was not sure if some computer hacker might not stumble on his research.

The laptop in his home-office was not connected to any outside sources. He would download website data onto a stick-file at the library and upload those files he wanted to his own PC at home. This was much safer and still functional for his needs. Had he become paranoid since his family had been taken from him? He didn't think so, but he wasn't sure either.

He knew he had evolved into a predator. *It was not a bad thing to be,* he thought. *After all, he was in control and monitored himself. If it got out of hand, he could rein himself in before he could cause too much damage.* These and many other thoughts passed through his mind as he drove to the Pine Street off-ramp and into Providence's skidrow area, the belly of the city.

 Skidrow in Providence is a historic site that was in its prime in the 1800's. It is comprised mostly of residential buildings along Friendship and Pine streets. Skidrow was made up of various cross-streets, on the southside of the City of Providence, off #95. It is a ten block long stretch of depravity. Low income families, light industry, bootlegged liquor and prostitutes make up the ambiance of this cesspool of human existence. Just one block northwest is a much cleaner, major commercial thoroughfare called Broad Street.

Collin found the local Salvation Army building and started to cruise out from there. He knew from experience that a drunk depended on food and shelter handouts to be able to maintain a standard of alcohol consumption. Within a block and a half, he found that source of alcohol in an unlicensed basement bar in a residential building. It was recognizable to Collin by the lack of children's outdoor toys and two small exhaust fans mounted on the exterior of the basement wall. They controlled the odors of stale tobacco smoke and washroom smells. The exhausts would not be found in a residential home and few families with kids would live above a bar. Collin's knew his fish would be in this bar.

The ideal organ donor is a healthy teenager, as well as people under the age of fifty. Being a long-time consumer of alcohol diminishes the organ's value. Those who have been drinking heavily for more than ten years were not considered good donor candidates by Collin's standards. Drunks under 25 years of age still had family who cared for them. They would search for their missing relative if one went missing. The perfect donor then, for Collin's purposes, was between 30 and 40 years of age; still reasonably healthy; not overweight and they could be of any race and either sex. At that stage of their drinking history they were often divorced or separated. They were all convicted drunk drivers, most of whom were no longer loved by immediate family.

In this basement bar, he found two ideal candidates, a man and a woman. Both appeared to be in goody health at about 28 or 29 years of age. Collin wore his dockworker's outfit and toque, which he kept stored in the trunk of his car for these fishing excursions. Having worked most of the night with Pattie, make him look tired, as if he'd been on a bender for a few days. Almost two days' growth of whiskers added the final touch to fit into this speakeasy bar as a customer.

"One of the guys at the mission said I'd find you here," he said to the bartender. He pretended to be out of breath from the two-block walk from the Salvation Army kitchen.

"Yeah and just which guy was that?" the elderly man at the bar asked.

"Jesus, he didn't say his name. I just stopped and got a sandwich and a coffee. My hand shook, so I spilled my coffee and he goes, 'get over to the white house on the corner, basement side door. They'll fix you up.'"

"The Sally-Ann Preacher was walking our way, so he kind of whispered the info," Collin said. His tongue ran over his dry lips and he tried to look like a lost soul.

"Well we don't allow just anyone in here. What did this guy look like?" the bartender asked.

"He looked like you and me, white…, you know, about so tall" and Collin put his shaking hand at about his eye level. "He's bald with a few missing teeth, like…." He just stood there as though his words were not believed.

The girl who Collin thought would be a good donor spoke up. "Hell, Jim, that's Mikey he's talking about. Let the poor bastard have a drink before he shakes himself to death."

"Alright, what do you want? You pay up before I serve you. Don't name anything fancy. I don't mix drinks, I just serve them," Jim the bartender said.

"I'll have a double rye, water on the side and don't cork the bottle. Here's a twenty and I got more when that runs out." Collin said, like a big man now that a drink was forthcoming.

The girl who spoke up said, "Hi, I'm Angie and this is my co-worker Sandy. We work at the post office when we aren't playing hooky like this. Come and sit with us. Move over Sandy, give my new friend some room," she said.

Sandy slid his chair to one side and Collin sat on the empty chair between the two.

"Thanks for the invite and the help over there. Mikey said this was a good place," Collin said.

"What's your name?" Sandy asked.

"Oh, yeah, I'm Paul, I just got fired over at the dock. The gang boss said I missed too many shifts or something like that," and he downed the rye shot before slowly sending down the water to put out the fire that was now roasting his guts.

"Hey Jim, set them up for the three of us, what are you guys drinking?" Paul asked.

"Double rye shots are just fine Paul, thanks a lot," Sandy and Angie both said in unison. Digging out two more twenties, he gave them to the barkeeper in reserve. Paul was their new friend now and he was buying. The day was young, the new friends were happy, and the booze flowed freely. There is a God. Why did they ever doubt it?

After downing the first three shooters, Paul asked where the toilet was. He was pointed to a co-gender room off the end of the bar. As he passed Jim the bartender, Jim gave him the once-over with a look of disgust. Why did drunks have money, while he had trouble paying his rent. Working in this crap-hole for peanuts didn't improve his mood one bit.

It was Collin's intent to get to the washroom to purge his stomach of the six ounces of liquor burning in his belly. He had no intention of allowing liquor to interfere with his fishing. He needed to be sharp and alert.

The toilet he entered was much like the room he left, smoke-stained, generally unkempt and dirty. It smelled of too many customers who had poor aim, so the toilet and floor were yellow with urine stains. The linoleum had the same pattern as the bar area, well-worn and needing replacement. A single 40-watt light bulb hung from the ceiling with an on/off string dangling on one side. The small window was open, and the exhaust fan sucked out stale air. It left no warmth in the room. In fact, it was almost freezing.

Collin realized that the entire bar operation only used half the basement of this old Victorian mansion. An area about 20 by 50 feet. There were half a dozen customers enjoying the ambiance. The prices were about 15% less than the other legal bars in the area. Nothing attracts a drinker more than cheap prices. It can be a shithole for décor but as long the booze is cheap, the customers will keep coming back.

When he returned to their table, fresh drinks were being set up and Jim put the last five dollars in change on the table beside Paul. When he just stood there, it was obvious he wanted a tip. Paul, now an accepted patron, slid the change to the side and said, "Help yourself, old man, have a drink on us."

Within an hour, Paul had heard the sad stories of both their lives. Sandy and Angie each competed to get their story out before the other. Drunks are like that. Given a little lubrication, their tongues can't stop wagging. It was considered a badge of distinction to have more DUI's than the next guy. Little did they know that it elevated them to the top of Collin's donor list.

While Sandy went to the toilet, Collin arranged to get their email addresses from Angie. When he had both emails and a sample of their DNA from the cigarettes they chain-smoked, he left. He put a twenty on the table and told them he was going home to Boston for a week, to see his elderly mom. He would email them when he was to return.

Collin stopped at Pawtucket, just north of Providence to add a few more fish to his donor list. Using the same strategy as on his other fishing trips, he collected three more donor's names, two women and a man. He preferred women because they were easier to handle once they were caught. They were, however, far more difficult to deceive. They are suspicious by nature and leery of strange men offering them drinks.

Very few drinkers are employed as hookers, however, they are still the easiest fish to catch. Hookers tend to prefer drugs, which Collin was not into supplying, even though he had access to the purist and most potent available. He could obtain or prescribe opioids and chemicals to his heart's content. Doing that would create a road a mile wide, leading to his door. Better to continue with the tried and true, given his prime targets were drunk drivers.

He had been using a few drugs to take the edge off his own nerves these past two months. Nothing too strong, just a little Valium once or twice a week. He had pocketed a fellow doctor's prescription pad whose signature was easy to duplicate. Her name was Dr. Sue Lo and she conveniently had her medical ID number printed on top of each prescription form.

Through Sid's contacts, Collin had acquired a fake driver's license, stolen registration and plates for his car. His aka of Paul Mathews was now firmly established. He obtained a police detective badge from a local pawn shop and had an ID card made in the same bogus name. He kept the new documents hidden in the trunk of his Lexus along with a set of brass knuckles and a Billy-club. These were for self-defense and he hoped he would never need to use them. He followed his alpha personality traits; be prepared and think of every possible hiccup that could arise.

Collin knew that in time he would need an escape plan from the police. He planned to have a stash of cash, a passport, an offshore hideout and perhaps even cosmetic surgery to change his face. He put those thoughts on the back burner for the time being. Collin didn't believe that his activities, collecting lost souls from skidrow bars had been noticed by anyone. There had been no mention in any of the local newspapers he had reviewed. He listened intently for information on radio-talk shows, whenever he was driving. No one was aware of the people he collected. They were the lost and discarded by society.

* * *

Within a week of his return from Rhode Island, Sid notified him of the urgent need for a pancreas and kidneys. They happened to be of a blood and tissue type that matched his new friend, Sandy in Providence.

Sending off an email to Sandy from the library in Newton, Collin, aka Paul suggested meeting with him in Providence. Sandy agreed to a private meeting at the Kingfisher Tavern near the Seekonk River, on Pitman Street. Collin told him he had a plan to make some easy money which he would share with him.

Sandy's short texted message reply came back that afternoon, "Great, your dime." Collin could see that greed was the right bait for this fish. With a few whiskeys and the greedy desire for easy money, he would reel this fish in.

Arriving at the Kingfisher Tavern 20-minutes early allowed Collin time to case the place. He found a booth in a quiet area, away from the pool table and juke box. The song currently playing was an old Merle Haggard song from the 60's, "Okie from Muskogee."

It soon became apparent to Collin that the machine was locked on one song that played in a continuous loop. When he asked the waitress about it, she just shrugged and said the Boatman's Bar was up the street if he didn't like it.

Collin's nerves and his mood were dancing like popcorn on a hot grill. His right eye had started to twitch by the time Sandy arrived. The constant use of self-medicated drugs wore Collin down and he was becoming more like the fish he patrolled for, than the doctor he was.

"Hey man, you sure can pick a shithole to meet in. This dive is pricy as hell and Dolly the waitress has the clap. She will give it to anyone, she doesn't care. Jesus, they're playing the same song as last week," Sandy said as he slid into the booth.

Collin resumed using his alias, Paul. He had four double shots of rye over ice sitting on the table. The one nearest to him already had the date drug in it. Sandy didn't ask, he just grabbed one closest to him and downed it. There were none of the usual pleasantries between old friends meeting after an absence. These were drinkers, plain and simple. Paul slid the drinks to the side and kept a clean one for himself to sip on. Spreading a sheet of paper out on the table, he smoothed the edges with his hand.

"What I have here is a plan to make some easy money this NFL season and if we don't get greedy, we could do the same with the hockey league," he said.

"I plan to skim a few grand out of Providence and Pawtucket bars this fall, and you can share in it with me. I need a front man to do the job because I'm busy doing the same thing up in Boston. Have you got a computer, laptop or tablet?" he asked Sandy.

Sandy was eyeballing the three drinks still on the table, licking his lips, he nodded. He then asked, "Just what are we doing that is so lucrative?"

"You ever play in a football pool," Paul asked. He slid a second drink to Sandy and waved at the bar girl for four more.

"Yeah. Why?" he asked.

"Then you know that if you pick the most winning teams each week, you can win big, like $500 to a G. With my scam, I pay the bar to run their pool. Every five weeks, I slip in my own player's sheet with a phony name that has the most winners and I collect the prize," he said.

When the drinks arrived, Paul moved them to his side and left one for Sandy. Still sipping on his second drink, Paul continued, "You following me so far?"

"How do you know which teams win?" Sandy asked. He was still eyeing the drinks. It was difficult for him to concentrate with full shot glasses of booze on the table.

"Simple, when I pick up the entries from the bar on the Saturday, I slip in one sheet of my own. I count the sheets and money and give the money to the bartender. He figures there are, let's say 67 players that week. After the games on Sunday I give him a breakdown of the standings. My sheet I fill in after the games are over. It will be a runner up for first place. After the Monday night game, I report who won, me of course and return all the sheets to the bar. I don't win at the same bar every week. I get a dozen or so bars signed up and rotate the wins, so I win from two different bars a week. Cool, easy money. Are you in?" Paul asked.

"Hell yes, when can we start?" Sandy asked.

"Look I gotta piss. You think on how we should split the money. Bartender gets 5% each week. I figured you to get 60% and you pay the bartender. I'll supply the software and get 40%. Think about it, I'll be back." Leaving the booth Paul saw that besides his own drink the only other drink on the table was the drugged one with the GHB.

After purging the three double whiskeys, Paul returned to the table and saw the GHB drink was gone. He waved to the barmaid for two more.

"Well, what do you think Sandy, is 60/40 OK with you?" Paul asked as the drinks arrived and he paid the girl with a handful of twenties.

"I think it should be 75% for me cause I'm doing all the work, going bar to bar. That's what I think," he said and downed his drink. He already had a plan for how he would rip Paul off and keep all the money. He was haggling just to keep the dumb bastard from catching on.

"Yeah, that could work. The pre-season games start at the beginning of August. So, you will still have a few months to set up your bars and get players to bet each week. You won't see any money for a while, so I guess that's a fair split. You pay off the bartender out of your share though," Paul said.

Taking a small sip from his drink, he slid the last one to Sandy.

"You finish that one and we can drive over to the library, where I'll make a copy of the computer program for you. It cost me a grand to get this hacker guy to write it up for me. Not to worry, I'll get my money back," he said as they left the bar.

Sandy was not too stable on his feet and he leaned into Paul as they walked to the car. Getting in, Sandy began to slur his words, as Paul turned up the heat and set the music to play a soft ballad. It was a big relief from Merle's repeated song of the last hour. Before they had traveled two blocks, Sandy leaned against the passenger door. He was out cold.

The drive up to Newton Highlands took over an hour following #95 north. Traffic was heavy for a Wednesday afternoon. Collin found that the music in the bar, coupled with the stress he was under made him jumpy. He popped two Valiums and drove just a little slower. His right eyelid was beginning twitch again. This happened when he got overly tired these days. Now, it happened several times a week and self-medicating did not resolve the symptom. He had a full night ahead of him, processing Sandy and delivering the organs to the Tennis Club in the morning. He would need a wake-up pill to counter the Valium that calmed his nerves.

When he got close to Dedham at about 1:30 that afternoon he pulled off the highway and entered the small town. Using the prescription pad of Dr. Sue Lo, he wrote himself a prescription for Benzedrine tablets. These would keep him alert for the next 15 to 24 hours.

As he approached the Lexus, he saw a young boy bouncing a tennis ball off the sidewalk. It hit the car window where Sandy slept and with no reaction from him, the kid bounced the ball again. The lack of response from the sleeping guy in the car intrigued the kid, so he threw the ball even harder. Paul flashed his fake detective badge at the kid and growled at the boy.

"He's a cop who worked all night. Wake him up and he will arrest you for disturbing his peace," aka Detective Paul Mathews said. The young delinquent just stared at Paul and his badge, gave him the finger and ran off down the alley. Paul looked about and saw that the exchange with the youth had gone unnoticed. Not wanting to draw any more attention to himself, he got into the car and drove back to the highway.

With wide-open eyes, due to the Bennies, Collin now picked up speed on the highway and arrived at his garage 20 minutes later. The trip had been almost uneventful other than the kid and he wished the remainder of the day would continue in this fashion. It was becoming more and more difficult to concentrate these days. Small things tended to escalate into more disturbing and challenging problems and Collin didn't understand why.

Getting Sandy onto the dolly was not easy work. His limp body seemed to weigh a ton although he was only about 185 lbs. and 5-foot-11. Collin thought again about installing a body-lift winch from the ceiling at the side of the garage. He could then lift the dead weight of his donors onto the gurney in a harness. The only thing stopping him was how to explain a body-hoist to his nosy neighbors. Running the kiln once or twice a week was problem enough, without the added stress of having to dredge up more explanations.

Before preparing Sandy for his upcoming operation, Collin put on his surgical gown and commenced the tissue and blood tests. Before the patient even regained consciousness, Collin knew the liver was damaged beyond use. Sclerosis of the liver was a common problem for heavy drinkers and Sandy was a prime example. The pancreas and kidneys were in good condition, as was the heart. Sandy's lungs were scarred and useless from smoking. Collin's lab tests showed that the major bones were salvageable. This last procedure of full bone recovery was time consuming, and Collin knew it. With the assistance of his newly acquired Bennies, he felt he was up to the task ahead.

The science of transplanting arm and leg joints had improved since the Afghanistan war. It was becoming possible to replace hands and feet in certain injury cases. Even a crushed leg or arm could have the bones replaced, preventing an amputation or the need for a prosthetic.

These developments created additional opportunities for Collin's organ donor fish to be even more productive.

Caution was essential, as hands with their identifying fingerprints were not considered safe body parts for the black market. The possibility of someone matching DNA from a donor organ from one of Collin's cadavers, then back to the police's missing person's report was a longshot. It was a part of the risk he had to deal with, and his stress level grew steadily as months turned into a year.

Even the removal of organs had become streamlined. What once took Collin hours to do in the first months of his clinic, now required only minutes. In Sandy's case, he just administered the heavy dose of sedative and let the heart continuing to pump.

Collin make an incision between the 2nd and 3rd rib, from shoulder to shoulder. This was followed by cutting the 7 ribs on both sides, from the armpit to the waist. He now had an electric bone saw to make this work easier. Any major vessels severed in this procedure were clamped off or cauterized. Collin then made a shallow incision across the abdomen, being cautious to avoid penetrating the large intestine. The last procedure was to use the bone-saw again to sever the sternum at the top of the ribcage. He was then able to lift the complete ribcage from the donor to expose the full chest cavity.

Since the liver was damaged, he removed it and prepared to retrieve the kidneys with the pancreas attached. These he placed in his new blood recirculation support station to maintain the flow of warmed, oxygenated blood to the removed organs. This newly purchased equipment gave him added time to recover more organs. He could now keep them sustained for much longer than using his old system of packing them in ice. The cost of the new machine to warm and re-oxygenate blood had cost him dearly. If anyone thought he was in the business to make money, they were badly mistaken.

It was now 8:00 p.m. and Collin felt the burden of his one-man task. He had been swallowing Bennies like candy to stay alert. These were followed by Valium to relieve the twitching of his eye and his shaking hands. He was building a wall in his psyche with drugs to protect his sanity, but he was failing miserably. He kept hearing his daughter Sylvia's voice call to him as he worked the long hours in his clinic. From time to time she even appeared to him, standing quietly in her hospital gown, at the foot of the gurney.

"Daddy, daddy, why is there so much blood." Sometimes the voice would say, "Don't let the blood go down the drain daddy." He knew these were his own thoughts being projected to take the form of warnings from his eldest child. He loved his children and missed his family to the very core of his being. The drunk driver who killed them had been released with nothing more than a slap on the wrist. Collin was now administering the punishment all drunk drivers deserved.

He struggled with the voices and fought to regain control. He was only halfway through the work planned for this evening and his mind was in turmoil. He needed to relieve the stress, since the drugs were no longer accomplishing the task.

Continuing with the operation, he connected Sandy's blood flow to the new transfer pump before stilling the heart with sedatives. He quickly removed the heart and connected it to the fresh blood circulation system also. With all the salvaged organs now on their own artificial support, it was time to start the major bone and joint retrieval.

This would be a two-stage process. Firstly, the bones and joints needed to be separated from the surrounding muscles and tissue. They were then chemically cleaned of all but the bare bone unless it was the joints he was targeting for re-use. These, with the tendons still attached were placed in a nutrient bath, then chilled in ice for transport.

Doctors who repair femoral neck fractures and hip transplants use the materials he gathered from the head and neck of the femurs. In addition to the eyes, Collin now salvaged the dura mater encasing the brain and spinal cord. The brain was donated to medical hospitals for training practice of the interns. Little of the donor's body went to waste in Collin's modernized clinic.

In all, it took until 1:35 in the morning before he was finished. Setting the timer on his kiln for three hours, he loaded the unused cadaver parts into the stainless-steel tray for cremation. The removed organs were safely being fed warmed, re-oxygenated blood overnight. They would be disconnected from the fresh blood and loaded into iced containers in the morning. The trip to the Tennis Club took 45 minutes and then the organs would be on their respective routes to deserving recipients. They would be in the warmth of their new bodies within four hours of leaving his clinic.

That morning, as Collin awoke from his sedated sleep, he was sure his daughter stood at the foot of his bed.

"Sylvia, what are you doing here?" Collin asked before his mind was sufficiently clear to realize it was an apparition.

"Daddy, they're looking for you and they don't think you are a very nice man. Why are they doing that, Daddy? Why don't the police like you?" she asked in her whispered child's voice.

Before he could answer, she evaporated into the wallpaper that his wife had so lovingly decorated their bedroom walls with. What was happening to him? He knew better than to believe in ghosts. These were signs of stress and they were becoming more and more difficult to ignore. He subconsciously wanted the visits from his child to continue but he knew the danger of permitting the fantasy to continue. He would need to research the subject on the library computer soon, before he became a wreck.

Chapter 7

THE NOOSE TIGHTENS

Lieutenant **Farnsworth swung** his lanky frame out of his double bed. It had been a sleepless night, tossing and turning as images of the missing people invaded his dreams. He would wake up to grapple with the conundrum of the MPs until he was exhausted. When he fell back to sleep, the cycle continued to repeat itself.

He knew from experience that he was becoming too involved. It wasn't healthy to get overly attached to one's case files, as they can dominate a cop's life. He needed a distraction. His mind went to Lorraine Simms, the woman who ran the counter at the Dolly Parton Dry Cleaners.

She was close to his age, about 38 or 40, large-boned with a figure that Cody found attractive. At just under six feet tall, she wore her blonde hair in a ponytail, off center at the back. He liked what he saw and overlooked her habit of dressing younger than her age. He didn't perceive it as vanity. She was a woman who wanted to feel young, even if she had to achieve that in a superficial way. Lorraine had seemed receptive to his flirting when he picked up his weekly supply of dress-shirts. It was time to take the leap and ask her for a date.

Cody arrived at the precinct by 7:30 that morning, checked his emails and call messages before heading to the bullpen for the 8 o'clock dayshift summary. It was Monday, so there would be the weekly show and tell session. That was what the precinct officers liked to call Captain John Evenly's open-case discussion forum.

The Captain's policy was that any officer on a difficult case was to present the evidence for review to all the staff. The intent was to generate new ideas outside the box, thereby injecting life into dead-end cases.

Today Cody planned to present his latest MPs data, received from around the state. He also had a missing person's file from Rhode Island now. He had developed a map of the Northeast that included all missing persons who fit the profile of the Eastie precinct disappearances. These consisted mainly of men and women, 25 to 50 who had several DUI convictions and were considered heavy drinkers. Since his search for more distant cities and states, the numbers had risen to over 50 conspicuous disappearances and possible deaths, mostly from the five slum areas of Boston.

The dayshift summary had followed its usual course until the Staff Sargent's agenda had been dealt with. He had issued warrants and person of interest requests from other precincts, as well as statewide arrest warrants. Cody was the second detective to present his case for review by his peers. The discussion was lively.

"I would suggest you draw a circle that contains all the Boston-area missing to see if a common or predominant, intersecting location emerges," came one suggestion.

"You know what I mean? A circle a few miles across, around each person's last seen location. Look to see where they all converge," the officer suggested.

"When did you first discover the DUI connection? It is not part of the questionnaire on missing person files," someone else asked.

"That connection came to light after a guy was suspected of having jumped from the bridge into the Charles River," Cody replied. "I checked the other missing person's files and filled in the information from the court records."

"You should create a spreadsheet with all the data you have on the 50 people to see if there are any other common denominators," the Staff Sargent suggested.

"Good point, I'll get on that after this meeting," Cody replied. It went very well. Another twenty minutes of brainstorming and he would have his work cut out for the next week.

"Have any body parts turned up? You know, just feet or hands," a female detective asked.

"No. Not so far, but I check every day for possible links. I have obtained dental records from the few victims who frequented a local dentist. Other than that, there is little to no DNA evidence available from these people. They are like ghosts and their lifestyles are not open to scrutiny. I managed to get a few potential DNA samples from hairbrushes of some of the women and shaving gear of the men. I have not gone to the expense of having them DNA-tested yet," Cody said.

"Lieutenant, proceed with the analysis on the samples you have for DNA. That way we have a record of in-hand evidence to compare against any DNA evidence we receive from other sources," Captain Evenly said.

Once the Captain had spoken, the steam seemed to escape from the gathering. They assumed the session was over for Cody and waited for the next detective to present his case. At times, Cody secretly wished he could gag the Captain. The group had some good input this morning, prior to the Captain's interruption.

Cody's first task was to get a few photocopies of his map from the print shop across the street. Businesses such as the Copy Shop had opened since the yuppies started to move into area. Most notably around the waterfront at Eagle Hill and Maverick Square. The whole of Eastie had been predominantly Irish, then Jewish, followed by Italians and now Russian immigrants for the past few years. With the arrival of young professionals, condos began to sprout up, which slowly dissolved the seediness of the area.

Scribing 10-mile circles didn't show much but reducing to five-mile circles around the city did. He added the towns where MP's occurred. Those from the outskirts such as Medford, Cambridge, Waltham, Quincy and even the new one from Providence were included, with even larger circles.

Cody found a connection between all the circles where they connected in the Newton area. It was not hard evidence. It merely put the 50 cases in an inter-connecting corridor. On its own, this information was useless, just one more egg in the basket. Eventually there would be enough eggs to fill the basket and he would have his villain. This was assuming there was indeed foul play at work here.

Cody's next task was to input the data from each missing person case onto a spreadsheet. He had a wealth of convoluted information on each case with a timeline of when they went missing. Over the next few days, he incorporated his information onto the computer he shared in the detective pool. He was clearly not a fast typist and his computer skills were self-taught. When he ran into trouble, he searched Google for help. Slow but steady, the information he detailed became etched into his mind.

As the spreadsheet developed, he noticed that there was information missing relating to personal habits. Much more was missing than he had realized before building the spreadsheet. The Staff Sargent's suggestion to develop a spreadsheet was proving to be extremely valuable. What missing information he was able find himself was gathered quickly. To acquire info from other jurisdictions and out of state, he followed procedure and enlisted the Captain's help. The process was slower this way but ruffled fewer political feathers.

His spreadsheet revealed that the missing people were without family ties. They tended to be loners who used alcohol as a crutch. Their families had given up on them and they had given up on themselves.

Most of them were in fair to average physical condition, despite their lifestyle. They ranged in age from 25 to 45 and had a 5 to 10-year history of drinking. Most were unemployed and had been throughout their alcoholism. Those who did work, had mediocre, low-income jobs where attendance was more relaxed.

Assuming the missing people on his list had met with foul-play, some common links should be jumping out at him. Who would benefit from the people who went missing? The word psycho came to mind. Someone with a grudge, perhaps? A satanic cult looking for disposable people to sacrifice. It seemed a bit of a stretch of the imagination, but it had happened before.

Maybe it was some nut who made lamp shades out of human skin. The options were as plentiful and twisted as what the human mind could conjure up. Cody remembered the college kids who a few years earlier, had beaten homeless men senseless, just to post the bloody fights on a U-tube video.

"Cody, got a minute?" Priscilla, the cute brunette from the detective secretary pool asked. The Lieutenant had been struggling for half-an-hour to do datasheet sort by category. He was short-tempered and reacted with the low growl you might expect from a cornered wolf.

"Yeah, make it quick," was his reply.

"Jesus love, I didn't mean to poke you with a stick," she said.

"I'm sorry Priscilla. This damn computer has a mind of its own and won't do what I want. Do you know how to sort by different columns?" Cody asked.

"Yeah, sure. Here, put your curser on the top, like this and hold down the mouse button as you drag down the column. See, like this." She leaned over him to demonstrate. Her perfume was intoxicating and the warmth of her breast against his shoulder made him uneasy. He was getting an erection for God sakes!

"Oh. Yes, now I understand," he said. Rolling his chair back from the computer desk, he pulled a casefile onto his lap. He looked up into Priscilla's blue eyes, peeking out behind her glasses. She took a step back, conscious now of the intimacy of their contact. He was a man, rough around the edges but a handsome one.

When she slid her glasses down to hang on the gold chain around her neck, Cody's glance moved to her breasts. His body stiffened from the effect she had on him. His mouth was dry and opened unconsciously, as he stared at the nipples stretching the thin fabric of her blouse. Their eyes made contact, sending a message of unspoken desire that passed between them subconsciously.

Priscilla was engaged to Neil Lindsay, a forensic technician on the fourth floor and Cody knew this. He had attended their engagement party a month earlier and now he felt guilty. Guilt didn't stop his arousal, but it put a damper on any further flirtations on his part.

"What brings a lovely creature like you this deep into the bullpen?" Cody asked.

"I overheard a conversation at Topper's during coffee break and I thought it was a good lead for you on your missing person's case," she said.

"I'm all ears. Please don't keep me in suspense," Cody said.

"Well, two of the detectives mentioned that if these were murder cases, such as a cult-type thing, there may be blood in the sewage system that could be traced back to a source. Does that make sense to you?" she asked.

It took the Lieutenant a few seconds to grasp the simplicity of this idea. From the mouths of babes, he thought. If the Captain hadn't cut his dog and pony show short on Monday morning, he may have had this idea several days earlier. The notion of a mass-murderer grabbed at his very soul.

"Let's hope it not a murder case. Thanks Priscilla, for giving me this lead. When you see those two detectives again, let them know I'm a nice guy and they can come to me with anything that's on their mind in future. They don't have to wait for the Monday round-robin discussions," he said.

Priscilla hesitated, then turned on her heel and walked back to the secretarial area. As Cody watched her walk away, he resolved to ask that counter-girl at the Dolly Parton Cleaners for a dinner date. The sooner the better.

Once he finished sorting the data file using varied criteria, he came up with four common threads; physical condition, age, drinking history and DUI convictions. He took his printout to the Captain's office, hoping for a few minutes of his time. He knocked on the door-jam of Evenly's open door.

"Come-in Lieutenant. Take a seat. What's on your mind? Did you solve that missing person's case already?" Captain John Evenly asked.

"Not quite yet. I've got a little info that could be posted if you think it's worthwhile," Cody said and passed the Captain his spreadsheet for review.

"Interesting concept you've come up with," he said. He studied the document for a minute or two and he asked, "So, what's next on your to-do list?"

"Well, I would like this victim's profile to be distributed across our state and the three other adjoining states if that could be done. If everyone is watching for the same four key items when dealing with a missing person file, it would sure help me."

"Consider it done. Anything else this afternoon?" the Captain asked.

"Well yeah, there is one thing. It's a long shot but scuttlebutt suggests I check the sewage system for trace blood. By doing so, if we're dealing with murders, we may be able to trace the blood to a source. What do you think?" Cody asked.

"That's a long-shot alright and could cost a king's ransom. Tell you what, leave it with me and I'll see if I can find someone at city maintenance who you can talk to. Don't go getting city work crews testing catch basins around town yet. Just talk for now and find out the lay of the land and whether this is feasible. Get an idea of the cost and so forth. You know the drill," Captain Evenly said.

The Lieutenant left the Captain's office in a happy mood. After three days of busting his ass with that spreadsheet, he was going to get results. He planned to pack up his paperwork and head for home. One stop first though. He needed to drop his shirts off at the laundry and Lorraine Simms, the counter girl would be invited to dinner. Not maybe or sometime down the road, this very evening. Cody felt pumped now that things were moving along as they should for a change.

Lorraine was receptive and just happened to be free that evening. In her mind, if he didn't ask her out that day, she would make a move on him. He was cute in a rough and tough sort of way. She saw in his face that he needed to be loved and that he had a lot of love to give.

He picked her up when the dry-cleaning shop closed at seven o'clock. She wore a fresh blouse and skirt, which he assumed belonged to someone who forgot to pick up their laundry. He hoped she didn't keep a spare wardrobe at the cleaner's so she could go on dates without going home.

Their first date was an adventure for them, asking questions without being too forward. Cody had selected a little Italian place in Maverick Square for their first date and it had set the mood just right. Putting their best foot forward prevented them from making social blunders on their first date. They were not teenagers. Both were close to forty but neither discussed their age this early in the relationship.

By 10:30 they could find no more reasons to keep the lone server at his station. The restaurant had closed its doors at 10 p.m. and they were the last customers. Cody left a large tip in recognition of the good service and the privacy their server had afforded them. Lorraine noticed his generosity. She appreciated a man who treated other people well. It was only a first date, but she expected it to be the first of many to follow.

As they walked the block down the street to Cody's car, she slipped her hand into his arm and pulled herself up against his body. She shivered from the chill of the cool May evening and the effect of Cody's closeness. She felt secure and Cody felt as if he had just won the lottery. Lorraine was a little shorter than he was. She smelled damn good and her hair was not in that off-center ponytail style she seemed to like. When things go right, they seem to have a domino effect. He cautioned himself against being too optimistic or aggressive. He wanted this woman as a friend but also as his lover.

When they arrived at her apartment on Turntable Avenue, Cody walked her to the front door. He smiled his best smile and the chipped tooth caught the moonlight. Taking her hand in both of his, he thanked her for her company and asked if he could call again. Maybe Friday night would work for a movie and dinner? Lorraine took his big face in both her hands and kissed him lightly on the lips.

"I'm in apartment 208. You just ring my doorbell Friday night about eight. I'll be ready, sailor." She turned before he could answer and was through her front door and out of sight around the corner. *She kissed me. Damn, that felt good,* he thought. *"I'm in heaven. . ."* he sang to himself as he walked back to his car.

The next morning there was a flashing message light on his office desk phone. Most people hated to leave voicemail, preferring to switch back to the receptionist to let her write out their message. When he picked it up, he heard his Captain's gruff voice, "Call Armando Batista at City Maintenance," the message said and followed with a phone number. Then, "Don't piss away any money, get an estimate." Short and sweet. *It was going to be another good day*, he thought.

"Hello. Is there an Armando Batista there?" Cody asked the guy who answered the phone in the maintenance area of the city yard.

"Yeah, I'll get him. You want to hold on, it'll take a few minutes?" came the reply. Cody agreed to wait, and he could hear the phone receiver bounce against the wall as it swung back and forth on its cord.

Cody tapped his pencil absently on his notepad where he had written a few questions he wanted to ask. After what seemed like ten minutes, there was a rattle on the line.

"Hello, this is Arman, who's calling?" he asked.

"This is Lieutenant Cody Farnsworth of the BPD. I have a few questions about the city sewage that I need answered. Do you have a few minutes to spare?" Cody asked.

"Yeah, shoot," came the cordial but searching reply. He sounded curious, like he wanted to know why a cop wanted information about the city's sewage system.

"If someone was dumping a foreign liquid down a floor drain or toilet could you trace it back to the source?" came Cody's first question. Nothing like shooting from the hip to get to the heart of the issue straight off.

"Yeah, that's possible. In fact, that's my job here, to trace the gravity storm and sewage systems for polluters," Arman said. "What are you looking for?"

"Blood," came Cody's reply.

"There are all kinds of blood. Animals, such as chickens, pigs and cattle, or are you talking about hospital blood, like the humankind?" he asked.

"I'm looking for the humankind, but not from a hospital," Cody said.

"What the hell are you on about? I get the odd residence in some ethnic areas of town who start an illegal slaughterhouse. That can be hard to trace unless the volumes are large. Like three or four gallons to a barrel a day, over weeks if not months," Arman said.

"Why is it so difficult? Blood is not something you see every day, is it?" Cody asked.

"Look man, it's not like paint or oil that floats on the surface. Blood gets mixed into all the rest of the liquids and let me tell you, there are plenty of varieties down there, mixed into the sewage system. If you are talking about the storm-drain system then that's a whole different ball of wax," Arman said. "I think you had better get down here to the yard, so I can show you the storm and sewage collection maps."

Cody agreed to meet him after lunch and wrote down his work address. He had a dozen phone calls to make and he had to visit the estranged wife of the bridge jumper. Cody needed to learn whether the jumper's pending three-month jail sentence was sufficient motivation for him to jump. It didn't seem that a drunk would care one way or the other. Perhaps the idea of being separated from his drinking buddies was too much for him. Cody wanted an answer for every question that came to mind. Loose ends didn't make for good detective work.

The timing of his two o'clock meeting with Armando worked in his favor. Cody would call it a day when they were done. It was already Thursday and he wanted to buy a new sports jacket and pants for his Friday night date. All he could think about was Lorraine. He wanted to hold on to the sense of giddiness he felt but it was affecting his concentration at work. Twice today, he had to refer to his notes to see what he should do next. He felt like a bloody teenager.

"This is the main city trunk line. It runs twenty feet below the downtown streets. Out in the burbs, it is only 4 feet down," Arman said. The slang of his trade filtered into his speech. Arman, as he liked to be called for short, showed Cody how the gravity sewage and storm-drain system worked. He was not involved with the pumping station systems. Only the storm-drains that ran directly into creeks, streams and rivers before they got too deep.

Catch basins for both systems were used on every block or less, in populated areas. They were one thousand feet apart in the outlying areas. It was a complex network that required a computer to control the flows from all the pipes as they fed into the system. In some older areas, the two systems used just one pipe and those were fed to the effluent treatment plant.

"We don't say sewer anymore. Its grey-water for drains and blackwater for toilets and sinks," he said. *All very hygienic,* Cody thought. *"But it was still shit,* he said to himself, so as not to offend Arman.

"So, if I had a felon dumping blood down a toilet could I trace it back to the source?" Cody asked after the overview of the system map was finished.

"Not very likely. It depends on how far from the source you find this blood. It gets diluted darn fast down there. Blackwater from thousands of homes and businesses can dilute five gallons of blood like nothing. What type of blood source are you talking about? A slaughterhouse, hospital, mortuary, veterinarian clinic? Give me some idea what you're looking for?" Arman asked.

"Well, it may be a residential house with a floor drain of some sort," came Cody's reply.

"OK, I think I know where you're going with this. You got this suspect dumping a few gallons or less of blood down a drain to get rid of it. By the time it reaches our trunk line, it is too diluted to trace. It would be a few parts per billion. Like one small drop in a swimming pool. Let's say a guy in a cul-de-sac is dumping the blood. I could find traces in the catch basin a block away, maybe even a few blocks away. I still wouldn't be able to identify which house it came from. With paint and oil, we send a camera up the line and we can see stains that we can follow," Arman said.

"So, testing the dozens of river and creek storm drain outlets wouldn't show any traces then? Is that what you're saying?" asked Cody.

"No, that is not true. Well, it is in one sense. If it's raining, the chances are very slim to none, to get a trace. If it is a few days after a rain or an extended dry spell, there is a slight chance, providing the volume is sufficiently large, such as an amount you might find in a slaughterhouse." Arman said.

Cody's eyes clouded and Arman knew he had lost him. "OK, like two, three hundred gallons. Now do you understand?" he asked. He was getting to like the big detective. He was smart and didn't seem to know it.

"Is there a difference between human and animal blood?" Cody asked.

"Chemically or something like that, yes I guess there is. Why does that matter? Are you looking for an illegal hospital?" Arman asked.

"Yeah, something like that. We can't say just yet. It is early in our investigation. How much would it cost if I got you to take a water sample from say twenty different sites around the rural area? Like, if we drew an arc about five miles from downtown and you spaced those samples out evenly along that line?" Cody asked.

Looking at the map, Arman worked out the time it would take and casually said, "$1,500 and you supply the test tubes, labels and map showing the test-location numbers. Oh, and you do the test work on the water. Do you want grey or black water?" he asked.

"For the moment, just hold off until I clear it with my boss," Cody said.

It was just going on five o'clock when he reached the Sears Roebuck store. Cody was no clothes horse, nor was he a dapper Dan. Just keep it simple and no plaids, he told the girl in the store. What he got, cost him plenty but Lorraine was worth every penny. The sports jacket was a light tan colored summer-wear suede. He found a pair of navy-blue pants that he liked and got them to sew the cuffs for him. They would be ready the next afternoon.

Cody whistled a tune as he strolled out of the store. To all the world, he was a happy man. He had a tie at home that matched the ensemble perfectly and a pair of brown shoes still new in their box. He just needed to be sure not to cut himself shaving and spoil the whole affect.

Chapter 8

WHEN THINGS GO WRONG

When **Collin made it back** to Newton Highlands after delivering Sandy's organs, he was exhausted. What he didn't need was his neighbor pestering him about some trivial nonsense. They were planning the spring block party and because his wife Tracy had been the chair of the organizing committee for the past five years, they were in a tizzy to get the file folders she kept, organizing the event. She used to spend days toiling in preparation for the affair. No detail was too small.

"Hi Collin, glad I caught you," Steve said, as he approached the car. "My wife, Sylvia, needs to speak with you. Something to do with the spring block party," Steve said.

"Is it that time of year again?" Collin asked. The year, since his family was killed, had not flown by for Collin. He had become numb to the passage of time. It would soon be the July, the month that drunk bastard had killed his loved ones the year before. This information added to the weight of the burdens already on Collin's mind. He slumped in his seat, exhausted.

"That's right Collin, another beautiful summer on its way," Steve said. It was then he realized Collin was slumped over the steering wheel.

"Look old buddy, I'll let you call the wife when you get a minute, OK?" he said.

I've done it again. I brought back his memories of the tragedy, Steve thought. I'll let Sylvia deal with him after this. Trying to talk with the fragile man was like walking on carpet tacks. That was not Steve's style and he wasn't good at it. He liked Collin and had adored his family. He just hoped Collin didn't come to the block party. *His presence there would ruin it for everyone*, Steve thought.

Collin looked up and realized he had dropped off to sleep for a second or two. As Steve walked back to his yard, Collin called, "I'll phone her in the morning. I have a kiln full of figurines to deal with tonight." Steve just waved over his shoulder.

When Collin got around to calling Sylvia, he had a full night's sleep behind him, without dreams or torment. Sylvia talked a mile a minute, as if her brain was on fire. She seemed to think that the faster the words came out, the sooner the fire would be extinguished.

Collin told her he would drop off the two file boxes the following afternoon, before he went on his hunt for more clay. His hobby was a good cover. It allowed him to travel extensively and gave him an excuse for his many absences. The gifts he gave his neighbors came from thrift shops and dollar stores. He passed off the junk clay pottery as his own creations. It was a simple ploy that worked and only required him to check that there wasn't a "made in China" stamp on the bottom.

Sid had sent a text message on his burner phone that a type B+ heart for a 97 lb., 13-year old girl was urgently needed. This request put Collin into high gear. He could use an organ from a female B+, B-, O+ or an O- donor. It should be a child's heart, although a small adult heart would do if necessary. The tissue leukocyte antigen type was the critical matching factor when selecting a suitable organ donor.

Collin's computer list identified Pauline Owens, a 27-year old woman who weighed 112 lbs. as a match. She lived in Nashua, New Hampshire, just 30 miles or so north of Collin's clinic. She liked to frequent a bar at the corner of Canal and Chandler, where she often sang karaoke. When she got drunk, she took most any man who looked safe, home for company.

Collin had danced with her once before and sang a few tunes with her. He had used the name Paul and declined her invitation to spend the night with her. He had promised her he would return if his relationship with his girlfriend turned sour. When he walked into the bar later that evening, she spotted him right off. She approached him where he sat at the bar.

"You still hooked up with your girlfriend, Paul?" she asked him.

"Nah, she split the night after I saw you here. Been trying to get back here ever since but my job on the docks got busy and they put me on night shift. I'm off tonight and go back on days, the day after tomorrow," he said.

"Oh baby, you got tomorrow off. Me too. Let's hook up for the time being. Kind of like we are free as birds as the song says. Come sing with me, I'm up next. Got a Tammy Wynette song picked out. You can sing George

Jones' part. You knew they were lovers, didn't you?" Pauline asked. "The song is The Telephone Call, OK?" and she dragged Paul off his stool. She was tiny but persistent and strong.

It was almost eleven before Pauline was ready to call it a night. Collin had to fake that he was hungry and wanted to go out for some food. Rather than lose him, she invited him to her place for grilled cheese sandwiches. She suggested he get some off sales to take to her home. He bought a fifth of rye for forty bucks from the bartender and then spiked her last drink with GHB. "It is one for the ditch," she joked.

They left the bar and were just about at Collin's car when all hell broke loose. Some guy stopped them, and he obviously knew Pauline, perhaps too well.

"Hey babe, I tried calling you at the bar to let you know I was slipping out of the house. The bartender said you was singing, so I left a message. How come your leaving early? We got a date, don't we?" he said.

"Hi Eli, this here is Paul, he's giving me a ride home tonight," Pauline slurred. The GHB was starting to do its work. In a few minutes, she would be out cold.

"No, he won't. If you need a ride, it will be with me," Eli said.

"Look friend, I'm helping this lady home so move aside so she can get in the car," Paul said with authority. Eli was having none of Paul's bossy ways. Pauline was his squeeze and Paul was an outsider. By then, the drug was taking effect and Pauline was becoming unstable. Paul pulled his wallet from his jacket pocket and flipped open his fake police badge and detective ID.

"Look pal, this girl is intoxicated and if you interfere, you go to the hospital and then I take her home. You got that! Your choice," Paul said and turned to face Eli full on. He was still holding Pauline up, but if it came to it, he would let her slide to the ground. With his brass knuckles in his hand, he grinned at Eli, invitingly.

Seeing the police badge shook Eli's resolve and he backed down. "What the hell, she isn't worth fighting over. You take her and go screw yourself," Eli said as he turned to leave.

"I'm dropping her off at home then I'm coming back here to settle up with you, shit-face. So, stick around, I got a fist full of knuckles just itching to reshape your face for you," Paul growled.

"Yeah, well, you're wasting your time man, I'm out of here. This place is the shits anyway. I'll be long gone in two minutes," he stuttered, in the toughest voice he could muster.

Paul pulled the brass knuckles out and waved them at Eli just before he turned away. The look on his face was pure terror when he recognized what Paul had in his hand.

"Just be sure you do leave, or you'll be kissing these," Paul said. The last thing he wanted was Eli going into the bar to report their confrontation in the parking lot. Collin didn't want to be remembered as having been with Pauline the last night of her life. He just hoped that Eli would leave as he said he would.

Collin got Pauline into the car. She was out cold before he pulled out of the parking lot. She said she lived three blocks down Chandler Street, so he parked the car in the alley on the next block. He waited a few minutes and made his way back to the bar on foot. He had to be sure that Eli had left. He had no intention of fighting, but he had to establish an alibi that he returned to the bar after taking the woman home. Most of the people in the bar were too drunk to remember who was there that night. Only the bartender would remember.

Walking into the bar, he took a seat and ordered a rye shooter.

"I thought you left with Pauline," the bartender asked him.

"No, she was pretty drunk, and her friend Eli said he would take her home. He said he was coming back here as soon as he dropped her off. I told him I'd wait and have a drink with him," Paul said.

"Man, you are the dumbest bastard I have ever met. She and Eli are an item. He isn't coming back here. He's between her legs right now, getting what you paid for all night," he said and laughed as he walked away, shaking his head in disgust.

Collin finished his drink and stomped out of the bar. His alibi was set in motion. When Pauline was reported missing, Eli would be the last person thought to be with her. Eli would tell the story of some cop in the parking lot confronting him. The bartender would remember some dumb bastard by the name of Paul. There would be ample confusion and in time, it would all be forgotten. Just another drunk, missing and presumed dead. All Collin needed now was to return home with the catch of the day while it was still fresh.

The 32-mile trip home to Massachusetts was uneventful until the lights of a New Hampshire Highway Patrol car signaled Collin to pull over. Pulling to the side, Collin checked to see that Pauline was sleeping soundly but still alive. GHB has been known to react with devastating effect on some people. Fortunately, she was not one of them.

"License and registration," the young night-shift officer requested. He had already attended a DUI accident and pulled three speeders over. This one was just a burned-out taillight but as the car stopped, he noted the break and signal lights were still working.

"Do you know why I pulled you over?" the patrol officer asked. Sometimes a driver will incriminate himself, by admitting they were speeding or had just smoked a joint. It was fishing but all is fair game on the freeway.

"I couldn't tell you officer. Why did you stop me?" Paul asked.

"Your taillight is out," he said looking at the driver's license Paul gave him.

"Mr. Mathews, Paul Mathews. What brings you out on such a late night from Newton, Massachusetts?" he asked.

"My wife's sister called to ask for a ride. She's under the weather. The wife and Pauline usually argue when

Pauline gets this way. Anyway, I was nominated to get her this time," Paul said.

"Is she OK over there?" the Officer asked. "Miss, are you alright?" he demanded. He shone his flashlight at Pauline, sound asleep with her head against the passenger window. Paul shook her by the shoulder and Pauline mumbled something incoherent about wanting to go home, to just go to sleep and that light hurts. The officer snapped off the flashlight and taking Paul's documents, walked back to his patrol car.

He radioed into base that the vehicle stop was OK. A safety procedure for all single patrol-car vehicles doing pullovers. He typed in the code link to the Massachusetts motor vehicle registration data bank on his computer. He got a blank page with the note: 'The system is temporarily being serviced.' Down again, third time this month, he thought to himself.

Making a copy of both sides of the driver's documents was all he could do tonight. He would write up the light-out infraction and request a confirmation of its repair within seven days. At least the driver wasn't drunk, although the vehicle did smell like a brewery.

"All clear Mr. Mathews, have a safe trip home. Sign this violation notice. It's just a warning. Get that light fixed in the next week and fax the repair confirmation to the number on the back. You might open the window a little in case someone else stops you about that taillight. You wouldn't want them to think you're intoxicated," he said, smiling.

"Thank you, Officer. You have a pleasant night," Paul said as he put his fake documents away. Being prepared for any eventuality was a trait Collin had picked up from his parents. Having false documents was just one of the many precautions Collin had put into place since starting his charity-drive for organ donors.

It was after midnight when he arrived home. He still had to process Pauline so that her heart would be ready for delivery by ten the next morning. His right eye began to twitch as he draped a blanket over the nude body on his operating table. He knew he would be visited by the ghost of his daughter if he didn't attend to his fatigue. Collin kept Pauline sedated while he ran the blood and tissue test-work. Once he was sure the tissue was a match, he decided to delay the removal operation until the next morning.

This heart was urgently needed. That was true enough. He was sorry that this donor would only be able to donate her heart. What a waste, with so many organ transplant patients needing help. Being a one-man operation placed limits on how much he could accomplish. He had to pick the low hanging fruit, so to speak and leave the rest to rot.

He kept her sedated and alive overnight. At 6:00 a.m., he began the heart removal procedure and by 8:00 that morning he was finished. Collin connected Pauline's blood circulation to his new recirculation pump and connected the ventilator to stimulate her breathing. He could now deliver warm, re-oxygenated blood to the body. Her brain was sedated and if there wasn't a power failure, he could keep the body alive without its heart for a few more days.

The removed heart was kept alive on the oxygen regeneration machine while he changed and had breakfast. According to Sid's last text message, the delivery of the fresh heart was a priority. Therefore, Collin left in plenty of time to deliver the cooler at the Tennis Club, when they opened at 10:00 a.m.

Collin mind was flashing thoughts through his brain like machine gun bullets. He still had the two boxes of files to deliver next door to Sylvia for the spring block party. As he drove to the Tennis Club, he tried to put his day's schedule in some sort of meaningful order. He hated chaos and lately that was the story of his life. Pauline Owens was also waiting for him as warm oxygen-rich blood pumped through her system, keeping the now still organs alive.

Collin needed to get to the library to use their computer. The National Organ Registry needed to know about the 27-year old type O+, 112-pound female who was unfortunately brain dead. She had all her organs available for transplant except for her heart. He needed to notify the bone-marrow, organ registries, eye and skin-graft banks about the available organs and tissue. No stone was left unturned in Collin's attempt to utilize every part of his current donor.

Even as his eye twitched, and the stress of his busy day stretched out before him, he hummed a tune as he drove. He almost hoped his daughter's ghost would revisit, as he reviewed the endless duties that required his attention today. A few more Bennies and Valium pills would keep him going. He had just pulled into his driveway after his visit to the Tennis club, when he saw Sylvia on her front porch.

His use of the computer at the library took far longer than he had expected. The library had recently installed timers on their computers. It was a money generating ploy that used old credit-card technology. You needed a credit card to activate the timer and you had to pay in advance. This created a paper trail that was unacceptable to Collin. It would be too easy for his internet searches to be tracked back to his credit card. He had not foreseen this dilemma, or he would have purchased a pre-loaded credit card in advance. He had considered getting one to pay for drinks in bars when he was fishing but so far, he had used cash.

He told the girl at the counter that he had forgotten his wallet at home. She begrudgingly accepted cash but had to set the timer for 30-minute intervals. Each time the computer timed-out he lost his search data. It became a time-consuming task that turned a two-hour Google search into four hours. He was not pleased and the girl at the library was only too happy to see him go.

His right eye twitched violently as he climbed out of his Lexus. He waved to his neighbor Silvia and said he would be right over. He left the car in the drive and dashed into the kitchen of his house to check Pauline's TV monitor. He saw that everything was operating normally. The ventilator was stroking up and down; the LED lights on the transfer pump and blood warmer glowed and the body temperature digital read-out showed 98.6 °F.

He quickly grabbed a porcelain figurine and found Tracy's two file boxes in the closet. He carried them all at once, over to Sylvia's house. With his hands full, he couldn't close his front door. It was a stupid mistake to leave the door open in his haste. When he returned ten minutes later, there was 11-year old Sharlene, Sylvia and Steve's daughter, standing in his kitchen. She was intently watching the monitor of Pauline lying motionless on the operating table of his basement clinic.

"So, Sharlene what do you make of that movie?" Collin asked. He was kicking himself for leaving the door open.

"It is pretty boring. Is this one of your operations at the hospital?" she asked.

"No, not yet. She is my patient and she is in the downtown hospital. I have this monitor so I can check on her from time to time. If you wait long enough you will see a nurse come into the room or the janitor will wash the floor. Neat, isn't it?" he asked her. His eye twitched and he tried to conceal it from the girl.

"No, it's boring. I'm going now to play with the other kids. Bye Dr. MacDonald. Be seeing you," she said and darted out the door, calling for her friends. Collin locked the door and went to the medicine cabinet for his Valium pills. *If it can go wrong, it surely will*, he thought to himself.

Collin was about to go down to his clinic after cooking a light dinner when his doorbell chimed. *"What now?"*, he asked himself? This day has been a disaster! Standing before him were three of his seven college poker players. It was Tuesday evening, Collin's night to host the game and they were the first to arrive.

"Best you pull your Lexus up further into the drive, buddy. Mike will never get his Dodge Ram, the pride and joy of his life into the drive," Cliff said.

"I was just about to make sandwiches for our game and completely forgot to put it into the garage. Here, take my keys and run it in for me. I still need to set up the table in the rec-room. I'll order in sandwiches from the deli instead of making them. I just lost track of time," he lied. He was getting good at it lately. Deceitful words rolled off his forked tongue like honey.

The evening progressed well as they played poker in the room his children used to romp in. Pauline waited patiently in the adjoining room, sleeping the drugged sleep of the dead. Collin had become adept at hiding his fatigue, partly because he had expanded the variety of pills he consumed. They were now a pharmaceutical cocktail of uppers and downers.

His friends were interested in the kiln and wanted to see it operate. Instead Collin gave them each a clay creation he had purchased to give to nosy neighbors. All too soon for some, but painfully late for Collin, it was 1:00 a.m. His poker friends finally broke up the game and left for their own homes. Collin had already swallowed three Bennies, chased down with half a dozen beer. He was in no shape to operate on Pauline and he knew it.

When the house was empty, he rode the elevator to the east side of the basement to check on his patient. She was resting well as he hooked up a new IV bladder filled with sedatives and nutrients to keep her quiet. He changed her diaper and replaced the catheter bag as he checked her vital signs.

She could remain like this for days, without damage to any of her organs or other transplantable parts. He would catch a few hour's rest before dissecting her further. With his new blood circulation machine and ventilator, his working pace was becoming less frantic.

It was quite conceivable, he realized, as he fell into a deep sleep, that he could keep several live donors sedated in his clinic simultaneously. They would be fed intravenously, like cocoons waiting to be opened to have their organs harvested. All it would take was money to buy the equipment. He could stack the bodies in tiers along the walls. That way, numerous, yet varied, common tissues and blood types could be readily available. He would no longer have to go on urgent missions to satisfy Sid's needs for specific donor types and he'd have a bank of fish in tanks waiting to be harvested.

Collin dreamed about his family that night. He wondered if the dream was triggered because his neighbor's wife had the same name as his daughter. He was probably just overly tired. Sylvia's ghost came to him with the same repeated message. She was going to tell Mommy about all the blood and the dead people daddy burned in the rec-room furnace.

She'd tell how he brought them through the secret hidden door into the rec-room and stuffed them into the brick fire box. It was hard for her and her brother Donald to play in their play area with all the clutter from his clay stuff. Now Emma wanted to play there too but there wasn't enough room for all three children. She said she was mad, and she was going to tell Mommy.

The dream disturbed Collin and he knew it was a wake-up call. He resolved to call Sid's underworld contact that very day. It would take time and money to prepare for a covert escape out of the country. He needed a passport to a country that would welcome a wealthy doctor with no questions asked. He had already chosen his new name. He would become Shane Mackenzie, a blond, blue-eyed descendent of an Irish father and a German mother.

Chapter 9

THE PURSUIT OF EVIL

Cody's date with Lorraine Simmons was like batting your first home run or smelling the sweet fragrance of a delicate flower. It was heaven and he reveled in the memory of that evening for weeks to come. It became his anchor to reality as he continued to probe the sick underbelly of Boston's skidrows.

The Captain had authorized five of the twenty sewage and storm-drain water tests. The Lieutenant now had to select the five locations that would give him the best results. The DNA of the hair and shaving samples were in after only a week's time. The theory that a cult or some maniac was butchering humans somewhere in the

Boston area was a longshot. The number of missing who matched his profile was now closing on fifty-five people.

"Arman, I only have five shots at this, and I need your help, big time. How do I select five targets and score a goal?" he asked.

"It's a crap-shoot no matter how you slice it. I like your idea of drawing the circular arc from an apex in downtown that you described. You already tried ten miles and five miles, so go the difference. Pick seven and a half," Arman advised. They drew a 7.5-mile arc radiating out from downtown center of Boston harbor on Cody's map.

"Now what? That's a lot of area to cover," Cody said.

"Sure is. I suggest we check only the storm-drain outfalls equally spaced around this arc. We start here in Hyde Park where the Cummins Hwy. crosses the Neponset River. There is a storm-drain outfall there that drains this whole area here." Arman hand was covering an area south of the city.

"Then I suggest we check over here, where Bridge Street crosses the Charles River. Then a little further up and east of downtown, at Newton Highlands. There is an outfall at Dedham Street on the South Meadow Brook waterway," Arman said.

"Yeah, now I'm starting to see what you're doing. Kind of like cutting a pie. We could test here and here," Cody said, pointing to two creeks on the north, near Saugus and northwest, past Medford.

"Will we be able to tell if it's human blood, if we find any?" Cody asked as they looked at the map.

"It depends on how close to the source we are and how much rainwater is in the drains. A negative doesn't mean the cult isn't in an area. It only means we didn't pick a good time to test. Water in a storm-drain flows about 1.5 to 2 meters a second or about 5 miles an hour.

"If it hasn't rained for a few days and we test when you think the time is right, say shortly after your culprit dumps the blood. Well then, we will get a sample of all the upstream water flow from an area about 10 square miles. Let's say we get a hit. If it is greatly diluted, then it came from further away. If it is close by then we can probably tell if it is blood from either a human or animal. A dump from only ten blocks away should contain DNA. Now, keep in mind, my information is based on how oil and paint react. Blood is a different kettle of fish," Arman concluded.

"So, if we get a hit, I know my perp is operating in that area. That is, if there is such an animal doing this stuff," Cody said.

"No, it only means that you found blood. It could come from a hospital, mortuary, vet clinic, to name a few sources," Arman said.

"We truly are looking for a needle in a haystack, aren't we?" Cody asked.

"I would rephrase that to looking for a needle in a whole county," he said.

The two men discussed their planned procedure for another hour. They set the time for the water tests to be conducted in the late morning or early afternoon. Cody said in all the recent missing person's reports, that people had all vanished in the evening. Cody reasoned that if they had come to harm, it would have been overnight. He would wait till he had a fresh case reported and if the incident took place after a dry spell, they would proceed. Otherwise the testing was on hold.

Cody didn't have to wait long. The small town of **Nashua** in New Hampshire reported a Pauline Owens missing. She had last been seen by an Eli Stone on Tuesday evening. He went to her apartment twice the next day and she didn't answer her door. When he finally got the landlord to open her door, the place was empty.

Eli was the main suspect in the case, according to Detective June Harper of the New Hampshire police. In his statement, he said Pauline was extremely drunk, as usual and in the company of a male police officer. This cop was dressed like a dockworker when he last saw the two together. An investigation was opened, and Pauline was added to the list of missing persons.

It was late Wednesday afternoon when Cody got the out of state response to his request from New Hampshire. This missing person met all four of his prime profile traits. As it hadn't rained all week, Cody planned to call Arman the next morning to schedule the testing.

"Yes, that's correct. She went missing Tuesday evening very late, around midnight," Cody said.

"Then we should have tested yesterday," Arman said.

"I meant we would test the day after I heard about the missing person. These files aren't opened until 24 hours after a person goes missing," Cody said. It was a small oversight on his part that confused the city waterworks employee.

"Fine by me, I'll go south at 11:00 a.m. and work my way following the arc north. I should have the last test by 2:30 or there about. You can meet me at the maintenance yard by 3:15 p.m. Should give you plenty of time to get them to your forensic lab," Arman said.

Cody was pleased to see some forward movement, even though it was a longshot. He called Priscilla and asked for her fiancée's private phone number at the forensic laboratory, upstairs. Neil Lindsay answered on the third ring.

"Neil speaking, how may I help you," came his polite response.

"Neil, its Cody, downstairs in the detective's bullpen. Look pal, I've got a big favor to ask you. I have collected some storm-drain water samples that need to be analyzed. Can you help me? It's a rush job and top priority," Cody said.

"With you guys, it's always a priority and a rush job. What is it this time?" Neil asked. His tone was no longer friendly.

"Hey Neil, hold your horses. If it wasn't for us guys down here busting our asses and shaking the bushes, your bunch up there in your lofty tower would be unemployed and walking the streets. You'd be out there looking for work, so cool it," Cody growled right back. He could be just as much an asshole as the next guy when he was pushed.

"Alright, don't get your ass in a knot. What's on your mind this afternoon," he asked. He had been in a bad mood ever since Priscilla had come home all hot and bothered a few days earlier. She was on about him not being more flirtatious like the boys in the detective's bullpen, for Christ sakes.

"That's better. I will have five water samples by 3:00 p.m. and I need to know if they contain human blood. If they do, then I will want a DNA-typing done, ASAP," Cody said.

"Look, if you were the Pope himself it would take at least three days. We're backed up a week up here. That's the best we can do," Neil said.

"Just do your best and I will show my appreciation for your effort at the first opportunity. You never know when you might need a cop on your side someday," he said and hung up his phone.

He remembered back 16-years, to when he was a rooky beat cop. Things were a lot simpler in those days. If the water was red, it was considered blood-stained and you sent the bastard to jail for the crime. Now you had to take the time to get things analyzed and catalogued. Dotting your i's and crossing your t's. *"It was a pain in the ass,"* Cody mumbled to himself.

This new missing person case from up in New Hampshire was getting interesting. The investigating officer reported the bartender remembered a guy who looked like a dockworker spending time with Pauline Owens. He said he was priming her pump and that the guy left with the girl and then came back to the bar a short time later without her. This dockworker guy said Eli took the girl home. The guy was quite pissed off when he learned he had been long cocked by Eli.

Then there was a very loose connection to a Paul Mathews with a sleeping woman passenger. They were stopped on the way home to Newton, Mass., fifteen minutes after the bar scene. The driver, Mr. Mathews, was dressed like a dockworker, wearing a peacoat and a knitted toque. The Nashua detachment of the New Hampshire Hwy. Patrol were on the job with this case. Not only did they read Cody's missing person's profile, they went the extra mile to tie in peripheral information. The road-stop for a broken taillight was a gift that pointed to Newton, Mass.

This is what the Lieutenant liked about his job. The facts on their own were convoluted. Put them all together like a jigsaw puzzle and then suddenly, ka-boom. You've got a picture, fussy maybe, but a picture none the less.

* * *

Wednesday morning.

Collin had just finished the removal of the last vital organs from Pauline. They were on the recirculation machine being preserved in their live state. He washed down the converted autopsy table, into the stainless-steel pan below. When he was finished, he opened the ball valve to flush the blood and small particles down the floor drain.

The image of his daughter telling him not to let the blood go down the drain flashed through his mind. He closed the valve once the tray was drained. He placed the rest of the body into an ice bath to ensure the bones and skin would remain fresh until he returned home from delivering the organs to Sid.

The Mass. State agencies of organs and body parts had indicated their need for what he had available. All they knew was it was a 27-year old female, type O+, who was gravely injured from an auto accident and was listed as brain dead.

Sid had contacts with the black market and the inside track to the National Organ Bank. He was very capable of feeding the organs into the legitimate pipeline without being traced. Never had a recipient's doctor refused an organ because they were suspicious of its origin. It was just taken for granted in the USA, that everything was legal and on the up and up. This was not Pakistan, China or India, countries notoriously guilty of illegal body part distribution.

Collin returned home that afternoon. He was tired and at loose ends and he didn't know why. Once he parked his car in the large double garage, it came to him. He saw his wife's empty parking spot and instantly remembered the blood going down the drain. If a city worker happened to be down in a catch basin, Collin knew that the size of the slug of blood he flushed down the drain that morning, would set off alarm bells. That was what was bothering him. His eye twitched and he broke out in a cold sweat.

He collected a few plumbing tools and a wrench from his tool bench. Armed with a bottle of bleach from the laundry room, he headed for his clinic. Establishing a connection from the bleach bottle with a small plastic pipe to the drain was child's play. Within an hour, he had jury-rigged a blender to mix the bleach with the water and blood going down the drain.

He also piped a small line to drip bleach into the collection tray below the body. He only needed a small circulation sump-pump to mix the blood, water and bleach in the tray before it was flushed down the drain. He would buy that with his new pre-paid Visa card at the Home Depot that afternoon. The only thing a nosy city worker might see now was a slight clouding of the water. Certainly, not red blood and not testable as human blood. Problem solved. He could now sleep easy.

Prepping the remains of Pauline Owens took him the rest of the afternoon and into the evening. He was so preoccupied, that he had even forgotten to eat dinner. The secondary transplant items were stored in their nutritional bath fluids, labeled and packed in separate iced coolers. These would be delivered to Sid via the Tennis Club locker switch.

Collin had been prudent in using the income received from Sid. Before the end of May, he would acquire four more blood rejuvenation machines. These would be connected to the new Hemosep devices that he had ordered from England. These new devices had been recently conceived, developed and manufactured in the UK. Collin's little clinic would soon become a process plant, providing quality organs to a deserving population.

Collin's eye twitch was getting worse by the day. Only last week he had been approached by the Chief Surgeon, and mentor, Dr. Luis Palmer.

"Collin, my boy," the elderly gentleman called to him.

"Good afternoon Dr. Palmer," Collin replied. His eye was again twitching, and he rubbed his face vigorously with his free hand, in a futile attempt to stop it.

"Come to my office after you have finished your rounds. I'll get my secretary to brew a fresh pot of that Columbia freedom bean coffee you like so much. OK son, can you do that for me?" the old man asked.

"Yes Dr. Palmer, I'll come by in twenty minutes." The two men went their separate ways, each with his own thoughts and concerns.

Dr. Luis Palmer was practicing his upcoming talk with Collin, to request that he take a six-month medical leave. Dr. Collin MacDonald thought about the twitch in his eye and how many Valiums it would take to quiet it.

Collin was in rough shape and he knew it. Burning the candle at both ends had taken its toll. It gnawed at him that the need for vital organs was so great. He felt as if he alone could supply the needs of the entire state of Massachusetts. When he arrived for his coffee with the elderly doctor his eye was quiet. His face was slack and emotionally drained of expression. Collin was as close to comatose as an awake person could be and still function.

"Son, I'm not going to beat around the bush here. I've known you since you were an intern here at this hospital. I was at your wedding, saw the birth of all you children and officiated over the death and loss of you family.

"It has been a rocky road that God has put you on and I hope you find the end of that rough patch of road soon. Until you do, I want you to see a good friend of mine. She is the best psychiatrist in the State, and she is an expert at helping people through what you are dealing with.

"I also want you to take a leave of absence from your duties here until you are rested and have a handle on your difficulties. There will be no argument from you. Agreed?" Dr. Palmer asked.

Collin had been contemplating handing in his resignation to the hospital. His clinic's workload had increased five-fold and the double duty at the hospital even at four-hour shifts, was daunting.

"I didn't think my condition was a cause for concern," Collin said. "I thought I was over-tired but chose not to use sedatives. You know how addictive they are." He didn't know just how obvious his lies and excuses were. His actions and the symptoms of his exhaustion had been reported to Dr. Palmer by every nurse who had worked with Collin in the past month.

"No need to apologize, Collin. We are all human and we all have a breaking point. You have reached yours much later that the average Joe, that's all," his friend replied.

The drive home from the hospital for the last time was filled with mixed emotions. He would miss his fellow staff members, doctors and nurses alike. Even a few of the cleaning staff had become friends over the 15-years he had served there. There would be an emptiness that he would have to fill by other means.

His clinic soon would be able to process five fish at one time. He even planned to see about getting one of those portable body hoists they used in some ICU departments. When one chapter ends, another one begins.

Chapter 10

LOOSE ENDS

When Cody came into work Monday morning, he expected to find much the same routine as he had in the prior few days. Hurry up and then wait for results. Hurry and wait. It had become mundane and when things didn't happen quickly enough for him, he became restless.

His date with Lorraine had been wonderful. They had kissed again and double-dated the next night with her girlfriend and her guy Martin. He was a cowboy, if ever Cody had seen one. Likeable, but everything was ma'am this and ma'am that. Chivalry was coming out of his yin-yang like a flow of soft honey. Lorraine didn't mind in the least. She was as passionate as a lady could be in a public place.

When they kissed goodnight on the front steps, he declined her offer to come up for a night cap. That motivated her to invite him to dinner on Sunday evening. He found that she was an excellent cook. She didn't decorate her apartment overly feminine or scent it with smelly potpourri or perfumed candles. She was the type of girl that a man could easily learn to love, without all the feminine clutter.

After dinner, she found her favorite George Michael CD and it wasn't long before they were dancing close, very close. It almost seemed as if it had been all staged, he thought later, as he drove home in the early hours of Monday morning. When they went to bed, she had a condom on him before he knew what was happening. She was hot and he was receptive. *"God, what a woman,"* he thought. This was a first for him. Usually, Cody had to work his ass off to get even close to scoring with a woman. It was a night to remember.

The next morning, when he arrived at his office, surprises were in store for Cody. Neil stood at the side of his cubicle, looking over the wall with a grin on his face. He waved a sheaf of papers at Cody and said,

"Here's another piece of your puzzle. On Friday, Priscilla told me about your missing persons case. I came in to analyze the water samples over the weekend. Here are the results," and he passed the papers to Cody.

"Jesus, thanks Neil, you're a God-send," he said as he reached for the results. They were more than he expected. The third test from the Meadow Brook outfall near the Dedham Str. was positive for human blood. The test on the seemingly cloudy drain water contained significant parts of type O+ blood and DNA that came from a white female. The other four tests were negative for blood content.

He had caught the brass ring, a hole-in-one, a slam dunk! Cody couldn't believe his luck. At the same time, it was bad news for the families of close to sixty missing persons. Their relatives were probably murder victims. Somewhere in the Boston area, there was either a psycho or cult operating.

Cody's informed the Captain on the water test results and begged off having to attend the Monday morning case review session. He then phoned Armando Batista at the city maintenance yard. They arranged to meet in the city works yard at 10:30 that morning.

Arman was as surprised as anyone that they had obtained positive results from the very first search. Having collected water samples himself, he knew that water did not show any visible traces of blood, not even the slightest, faint pink discoloration. He had searched for oils and paint before and chemicals used in crystal-meth production, but never human blood.

"How did they test for blood and DNA?" Arman asked.

"As per procedures spelled out by the forensic lab. They tried an absorbent paper-test and sprayed Luminol on it when it dried. That got nothing positive, so they used a wettest designed to test blood in urine, called Hermastix and that came out positive. They then separated the red blood and white cells to get the DNA results I showed you," Cody explained. "Apparently red blood cells don't contain DNA, only the white ones do."

"Well, it's a lot easier to trace oil and paint, I'll tell you. What can I help you with today?" Armando asked.

"Well now that you ask, I need to trace the blood to its source and that is where you come in," Cody said. "The lab said the blood was diluted with water and other liquid substances, to one part per one hundred. The samples you collected contained two ounces each. The amount of blood in your sample was 1/100 of the two ounces or .5 grams. How far from the source would cause that amount of dilution if 1.5 gallons of blood was dumped into the storm-drain at one time?" It was a question Cody had struggled with. He had no way to arrive at the answer. It required someone familiar with how much water entered the storm-drain system in the area that the test-sample was taken.

"Thanks. I opened my mouth to ask if you need help and man, you need a miracle. We have had no rain for seven days. The storm-drains are virtually dry right now. On Thursday, when I was down in those catch basins at the outfall, there was about a 5% flow. This is a guess, pure and simple. I would say that to get that amount of dilution, you would need to have 150 gallons of water mixed in with the blood. It would take an area from the test collection site about 2,000 feet due west and arcing north about 500 feet to Boylston Street. It is a big area that has about 1,000 homes in it," Arman said.

"Thanks Arman, I appreciate your help. You just gave me one hell of a lead with this information. I must go now. See you later," he said.

Cody tore out of Arman's office heading for his car. It was one thing to learn that people were very likely missing due to foul play. It was quite another to discover the perp's active crime scene in an allotted area of an east Boston suburb. As he drove, he made a phone call to the Nashua, New Hampshire Police Department.

"Hello, this is Lieutenant Farnsworth of the BPD, is Detective June Harper available?" he asked the desk clerk who answered.

"Please hold while I transfer your call," came the reply from the girl.

"Harper here, how can I help you, Lieutenant?" a pleasant woman's voice asked.

"Hello and please call me Cody. I'm searching for some 55 missing persons. One of them is Pauline Owens, who you have listed as missing. There are two things you may be able provide that would help me today," he said.

"You're over in Boston, aren't you?" asked June.

"Yes, that's correct. Most of the cases are in our area. Last month we discovered that missing people from outlying areas may possibly be connected to our case. Our profile on the case was reviewed by your office, who forwarded the Owen's data sheet to us. We now need more specific information to resume our search. Can you help?" Cody asked.

"Yes, ask away, I'll help if I can," she replied.

"Your Hwy. Patrol Officer mentioned a Paul Mathews and a Newton, Mass. address. Could you send me that address and a copy of the driver's license? The second request is for a DNA sample of the missing woman," he said.

"The Highway Patrol Officer's report can be faxed in a few minutes. The DNA will take some time to get," she said.

"Look, please don't go to any expense. Just send a hair sample from a comb or even a used glove that she had worn. Anything you can be sure she wore, will do. I'll have the DNA extracted down here," Cody said. He had not cleared this with his Captain, and he could already hear the whining from the mayor's office.

"In fact, please send it to my attention, collect via UPS. It makes it easier for all concerned," Cody added. He would see his boss in a few minutes to ask if he could request assistance from the New Hampshire police. A little after the fact perhaps, but he would ask and that would satisfy the instructions he had been given for acquiring assistance from his counterpart up north.

June transmitted the fax as they spoke. She would stop by the Owen's apartment in the next hour, accompanied by Eli, to ensure the collected DNA items came from Pauline. She told Cody that this Eli character was married and had become very cooperative after they informed him that he was their prime and only suspect.

When Cody got back to his cubicle, there was a message from the Captain that the detectives' meeting had produced a few more ideas relating to the MP casefile. He was to come by the Captain's office as soon as he got this phone message.

As he made his way through the bullpen, his fellow Detectives eye-balled him. A few smiled and some nodded. They knew something he didn't, and it made him uncomfortable.

The Captain's secretary ushered him straight into the Captain's inner office. The administrator, who had been reviewing budgets with the Captain, was asked to step out for a few minutes, while the two policemen discussed the MP files. Cody was not accustomed to high-status, priority treatment, so he enjoyed the moment while it lasted. It was like seeing sunshine through clouds on a rainy day, for a brief few seconds.

"Lieutenant, have a seat. The case review session went well this morning. I presented your case and now I will review the results with you." The Captain leaned back in his swivel chair, bridging his fingers in contemplation.

"First, those who had made suggestions last week were pleased that you got good results when you followed up. One idea that came up, was to look at the dates and times of the disappearances. You might correlate them on the spreadsheet to phases of the moon, weather, religious habits or things like that.

"Secondly, the fact that our victims are all alcoholics and have several DUI's may be key to them having been targeted. Someone may be holding a grudge. Check to see if any of our victims had been involved in traffic accidents. Could our perp be a vigilante seeking revenge against a drunk driver?

"The group concluded that there is a link between all 55 cases. Find the connection and you will find your culprit," the Captain said. Cody wrote notes at a furious pace. He used his own style of shorthand, all cops do. *The academy doesn't teach shorthand in their training sessions, but they should*, he thought.

Cody produced his map of Massachusetts and pointed out the water test locations. He then provided the Captain with a copy of the positive lab test for human DNA. Cody explained that the area the perp was operating in was quite large. It was a twenty-five-block square drainage area from near Newton Highlands that was of greatest interest. It encompassed approximately 1,000 homes and small businesses. Finding the killer in that large an area would be a daunting task.

"Is there some way to monitor the storm drains upstream of that point, to zero in on where the blood is being dumped? It would help if we had an electronic device to emit a signal when human blood is found in the waterflow," the Captain said.

"I don't know of anything like that. I'll ask the city wastewater guys and the university engineering department. Technology is progressing faster than we know. Anything is possible nowadays," Cody said.

"Good plan. Is there anything else I need to know?" the Captain asked.

"Yes sir, just one thing. The police up in New Hampshire have a full MPR on Pauline Owens. I will need a copy. All I have is the data sheet I gave you. I also want a sample of the girl's hair or something like a piece of her clothing I can test for DNA. It would be a big help," Cody said. "I don't want to create an issue with the Mayor's office again."

"Yes, go ahead with those two requests. Do the DNA testing here in our own laboratory? I suppose you will get help from the FBI on the driver's license photo?" he asked.

"That would be my next move, yes," Cody replied. He was asking for approval after the fact and he hoped that his deceitful little act would go undetected. His 16-years of dealing with criminals and cheats had taught him to lie like a pro.

When the hair sample and a glove arrived, Cody rushed them up to Neil without calling ahead. Neil had taken a sick day in exchange for working on the weekend and Cody cursed his bad luck. It was a Forensic Department cost-saving measure. Everything that cost money had to be approved.

It was a wonder anything ever got done, Cody thought. He left the articles to be tested with the clerk and asked to have Neil phone him when he returned the next day.

The fax revealed that the driver's license and address turned out to be bogus. The photo would be of no help until they apprehended someone. Cody's made a request to the FBI to cross-reference and search their records for a match. It was his last hope.

The FBI report on the photo came back as negative. They did not have a matching photo. This only meant that the photo was of a person who had not joined the military, been imprisoned, held a passport or worked for any federal government agency. The FBI had entered the photo into their database and would check periodically for a match. It was very likely the person in the photo had modified their appearance with theater-grade makeup. The FBI and Homeland Security seemed to have money to spend. President Trump had made sure of that, since he was terrified of terrorists.

Cody began updating his spreadsheet. He asked Priscilla to track down university contacts for information on an electronic device to monitor the storm drain water for blood molecules.

Chapter 11

EXPANDING THE CLINIC

D
r. Collin MacDonald, alias Paul Mathews, was acting like a kid with his dad's credit card. He had a shopping list for equipment to turn his clinic into a five-bed operation. Aside from his purchases from the UK, he needed a portable body-hoist and rolling beds he could mount to the wall. He didn't have a great deal of space to work with. The donors would be kept sedated and he was toying with an idea of storing them in a vegetative state. He still needed to do more research about brain death.

He scoured the used medical-supply stores on Jefferson Avenue and had the salesman load his purchases into his rented box-van. The van would provoke questions from his neighbors, but he was ready for that. He would say that he was clearing out articles that were reminders of his deceased family. Clothes, beds, furniture and toys had to go to ease his grief and pain. No, he didn't want any help, thank you. He wanted it to be a private, final, farewell to his departed family.

He found five ambulance gurneys to suit his needs as patient beds. Collin bought some three-foot long, heavy-duty wall-brackets to be used for shelves, from the hardware store. He planned to attach them to the cinder-block wall to stack three gurneys high, in two tiers. With the modified body-hoist, he could lift a donor and gurney off the wall and roll them to his autopsy table. There, he would use the equipment to hoist them onto the operating table.

It would be like the production assembly-line Henry Ford had conceived. As he worked, Collin failed to notice that the twitching in his eye was in remission. After three days of hard work building his new clinic, he was in a better mental condition that he had been in months. The manual labor had been therapeutic, but he hadn't seen the connection. The fact was, he had not been cutting up live bodies while the renovations were under way. This observation would not have been overlooked by a healthy person. It never crossed Collin's mind that that had been the calming factor for his extreme mental fatigue.

When Collin next went to the library to use the computer, he swiped his preloaded credit card to activate the timer. The computer would run all day now, without interruption. His card was debited for every half-hour segment that he used. He sent a coded message to the forger creating his new ID and passport and sent him a $10,000 email transfer from an offshore bank account.

He then did a search on how people become brain dead. The most common cause, after massive cranial damage, was the lack of oxygenated blood to the brain. He found that if he closed off the blood-flow in the two carotid arteries in the neck, he could induce brain death. He deleted his search history and email-account records, before shutting down the computer.

He restarted the computer to check for traces of his previous activities and was satisfied that none were left behind. To be doubly sure they were gone, he did several searches on mundane subjects to consume as much computer data as he had accumulated on his covert searches. This was to overlay new data on the hard-drive and erase the brain research information by imprinting over his earlier work. Once he surpassed that time, he knew the computer's hard drive had been wiped clean. He wasn't positive this would hide his research topics, but it was the best he could improvise. Satisfied, he logged off and left the library.

He was reasonably confident that he had covered his tracks. It would take one dedicated expert to dig up any trace of what he had been up to. They would need to know which computer he had used and predict what to look for. He had been this cautious with every aspect of his organ donor operation. He was invisible, he thought.

Paul Mathews had been collecting donors at a rate of one or two a week since January. By mid-May the number had jumped to three a week. Once he learned to streamline his procedures, by June, the clinic had five extra beds and the numbers now increased accordingly. Not having to work at the hospital allowed him more time to pursue his passion, to remove every drunk driver from the highways of America.

Sid had been very patient during the renovations. He didn't know what Collin was doing, only that he had been relieved of duty at the hospital. He understood that the doctor needed some time to organize his life. He kept the donor banks at bay for the week that he thought Collin was convalescing. Now Collin had told him he could begin anew the following week.

The only other interruption to Collin's operation was the upcoming Spring Block Party. It was being planned by his neighbors, Steve and Sylvia, for the middle of June. He had to attend. It would look odd if he missed it. He liked the seclusion he had established with the surrounding neighbors. They treated him with kid gloves, saying little and asking even less of him.

On the Saturday of the party, Collin showed up with a basket full of small pottery pieces. He handed them out as if they were gold and talked about each piece as if it was a treasure he had created. While chit-chatting with his neighbors, one of the children announced he would be taking his dad for a Big Mac the next day to celebrate Father's Day. That was the type of remark Collin was hoping for. He pretended to reflect on his deceased family. With his right eye twitching, he excused himself and made a beeline for his front door. Once inside he closed the drapes, sending the silent message to everyone, to leave the poor man to his sorrow.

Since the clinic renovations had been completed, Collin had not gone fishing due to the block party. Sunday evening, he left in his car, going east to the city of Worcester, population 183,000, 90% of which were white Americans. 10% of those lived below the poverty line and used alcohol to soothe their troubled souls.

Paul had emailed three recently convicted DUI drivers, suggesting that they could make an easy buck if they met him in the Horseshoe Bar and Grill over on Plazas Avenue. None of the three, two men and a woman knew each other.

He had met each person separately while on a catch and release fishing trip in early June. He knew their blood and DNA profiles as well as their personalities and weaknesses. He knew they would show up because they were all desperate and needy. They liked their booze but hated having to work to pay for it.

By 7:30 that evening the four conspirators sat in a booth at the back of the bar, knocking back Paul's booze, as fast as he could buy it. Paul used his tiny bladder excuse to purge his gut of alcohol several times. He had his victims convinced they would be millionaires before football season was over. As proof, he had shown them his data sheets identifying the various bars and the football pools he ran. The money was easy, the idea was clever, and they were devious.

By 10:00 p.m., they were on his hook, ready to be reeled in. Paul had suggested they go to a local drugstore to copy his computer disc and paperwork. Afterward, he would give each of them a ride home and he suggested they should all use the toilet before leaving. He wanted no accidents from either end of his fish once they passed out. He gave each one a slightly different dose of the GHB drug. He wanted the girl down first and in the front seat. He scheduled the dose for the other two, to pass out five minutes apart, in the back seat.

As they walked to the car, the woman started to fade. She stumbled and Paul caught her arm before she fell. The two men helped her get into the front seat. Within four blocks of the drugstore, the smaller of the two men passed out.

"Jesus Christ Mike, look at those two. They can't hold their liquor worth a damn. They're sleeping like babies while we plan the biggest score in NFL history. What a waste! I guess that means the more for you and me, buddy," Paul said. He could see Mike grinning in the rearview mirror. Mike grunted an incoherent reply and slowly slumped down on his side of the back seat.

The hour's drive home was uneventful. Collin knew the highway patrol required a legitimate reason to pull you over and he left no room for that possibility. Three people sleeping in a car on the highway at night was a common sight. Collin made sure all the lights were working when he switched to his bogus license plates. He kept the heat on and the music soft. There were the odd grunts and coughs but little else came from his catch of the day.

This was the first time he had caught multiple fish on one trip. The logistics of doing so were soon coming into play. He transported the heaviest man down to his clinic first. Using his portable body hoist, he literally dragged him from the back seat in the harness. Setting him upon the ambulance gurney was easy using the hoist. He rolled him into the house and down the elevator. Following this procedure, he soon had all three sleeping donors strapped into their individual slots, suspended from the cinder block wall.

Prior to making this trip, Collin had decided to render each of his guests into a brain-dead state, for his own peace of mind. Having five guests at one time would be considered a handful for a team of medical professionals. On his own, he was courting disaster.

After attaching electrodes to each donor to record electrical brainwave activity and heart rhythm, Collin applied pressure to their carotid arteries. On average, it required three to five minutes of concentrated pressure to both neck arteries before the monitor flat-lined. When the deed was done, their heart and lung functions were still regular. He installed a ventilation device as a backup. Loss of oxygenated blood flow meant the loss of the vital transplant organs.

He attached temperature and blood pressure monitors to each of the three cadavers, which he could view on the TV in his kitchen. He was pleased with himself to have three of the five vital blood types ready to donate organs upon demand. He could keep organs alive almost indefinitely with his new equipment.

On Monday evening Collin again donned the persona of Paul Mathews to go fishing. Tonight, he went north to Newburyport, a fishing town of 20,000 people, where the men worked on their boats and the women drank. Oh, happy days, Collin thought. These simple people had condemned themselves to a life of tedium and boredom. Their only escape was alcohol or drugs.

He had two ladies to pick up tonight, which could prove difficult, should a conflict arise between them.

Collin had a strong sense that the women would be inclined to accept his proposal for a threesome at his posh hotel suite. It was not a room but a suite, that boasted a jacuzzi, an exercise gym and a king-sized bed. A perfect setting in which to play out his fantasy. At least that's what he told the women the last time he met each of them separately for drinks. They pretended to be shocked, but he was sure they were interested.

Paul dressed a little more dapper this evening. He met Gloria first at 7:30 pm. Her man was off on a two-month halibut trip up in Greenland. He had just offered her a drink to warm her up for the evening's entertainment, when Tiffany, a real bombshell arrived. She was quite a bit taller than Gloria. They were opposite in every way, except for their fun-loving ways. Soft music played and the mood in the lounge was warm. They drank, snacked and took turns dancing with each other. By 9:30 they were ready for the next phase of the evening's delights.

Paul ordered a round of whiskey shooters. "One for the ditch", he called it. The two girls had one last dance to make sure they each wanted to participate in Paul's threesome fantasy. The GHB-laced drinks were waiting upon their return. It was down the hatch and off they went, giddy as teenagers heading to a beach party.

Paul told the women the hotel was over by the #95 highway, ten minutes west. They passed out before they got two miles down the road. He had caught two very fine fish tonight. Having to cut into Tiffany's sculptured body, would be a shame but he needed her blood-type to round out his organ menu.

Back in his double garage, Collin used the hoist to remove Tiffany from the back seat, then strapped her to the ambulance-style gurney. As both ladies had ingested the same dosage, he calculated that Gloria, who was lighter, could rest in the car for a few minutes while he delivered Tiffany to the clinic.

He took the time to undress Tiffany and shaved off some of her beautiful brunette hair to attach the electrodes for the brainwave and heart monitor. Upon his return to the garage, he found the garage door rolled up and wide open. Straddled on his mountain bike was 14-year old, Joe Freeman from the next cul-de-sac. Seeing Collin and thinking he had done something wrong, Joe panicked. His foot missed the bike pedal and he came down hard on the bar with his crotch. As his hands slipped from the handlebars, his body collapsed onto the driveway in a ball of pain.

"Easy son, don't move, just rest and let your heart settle down. It's the blood pressure in your groin from the shock of the injury that is causing your pain," Collin consoled him. "What are you doing here? It is almost 10:30 p.m. Isn't it late to be out on a school night?"

"My mom and dad are fighting, and I just took off. Did you know that my garage clicker opens your garage? Some of the guys at school said this could happen if you tried enough doors. I'm sorry, I didn't mean any harm. Is that lady sleeping in your car OK?" Joe asked.

"Yes, she just had a little too much wine with her dinner. I left a message at her home to let them know she'll be sleeping on my sofa tonight," Collin said. "Would you like me to get you a glass of water?" Collin asked. Joe was starting to recover from his painful injury and was now sitting up on his backside on the pavement.

"No. I'm OK now. You're right about just relaxing. The pain stopped quicker that way. Boy, wait till I tell some of the guys at school how to reduce the pain like that. I'll be a hero," he said.

"Well, if you're sure you're okay, I should take care of my friend. Good night, Joe. I think it's safe for you to ride home now. You shouldn't ride your bike at night without a headlight and reflectors," Collin said. "Want to close the door with your clicker to see if it works again?"

"Yeah, that will be cool. Thanks Dr. MacDonald," young Joe said and pressed his clicker to activate the door mechanism.

Collin checked to see that the boy had indeed leaving the area before he ducked under the closing door. He pulled the plug that powered the door system, once it was closed.

"What you don't learn from a child," he muttered to himself. That was a close call. What if one of his nosy neighbors had been going by while he had a 185-pound man on his portable body hoist? It could have been a disaster. He made a mental note to buy a new, secure door remote in the morning.

The prep-work, to get blood and urine samples tested from the last two fish, took the better part of the night. He only had to place them into a comatose state. He quickly stopped the blood-flow in their necks from reaching their brains until the monitor showed a flat-line. Finally, he placed them on ventilators and blood-pressure monitors before stacking them on the wall-mounted shelving. At long last, he was going off to bed by 5:30 a.m.

Sid's text message on Tuesday morning requested a liver for a female patient at the Boston Central Hospital. She was an O-positive blood type and Collin had a perfect match from one of his five new fish. It would be the first of many organs to be ordered and delivered the following days. This first organ was Tiffany's gift of love, since she was the first donor from the new, enhanced clinic.

Chapter 12

LIKE DOMINO'S

The Lieutenant was excited about the blood find in the storm drain system. There had been two and sometimes three MPRs each week for the past months. Now, they suddenly stopped.

The blood they found in June belonged to Pauline Owens, which prompted the Mayor to give Cody his full support. It was all he could do to keep the politician from going on TV to warn residents to keep their doors locked. Nothing like announcing that a killer is on the loose in the Newton Highlands area to create panic and chaos in the community.

Cody had found no simple device to monitor the storm drains for blood. When it rained heavily a few days after the first find, they again found blood traces in the same location. They knew the drain had just been flushed because the DNA was the same. It was an eye-opener for Cody. He now understood that blood could sit in a section of drain for a few days if there wasn't sufficient water to wash it away. It took rainwater to deliver the blood downhill to the catch basin and then onto the outfall at the creek.

In the second half of June, there were five missing-person reports within two days. What was going on? How could a psycho or cult snatch that many people in two different locations without a trace? Cody didn't believe in the supernatural, but this was getting close to being just that. It was downright scary, like being in the twilight zone.

During lunch at the greasy spoon across from the precinct office, Cody laid out his spreadsheet and map for Jamie Fitzpatrick, a fellow detective.

"This one here, who is it?" Jamie asked. Pointing at the list of names.

"Jim Fairchild. He is the only one that at first, looked like a jumper," Cody replied.

"You show here, under physical evidence, skin fragments, stretched coat fabric, partial thumb print and a Lexus floor-mat fabric. That's not bad, given the early stage of the missing persons cases. His is the only extensive evidence of foul play found, right?" Jamie asked.

"Yeah, there are a few hair samples and DNA from other MPs, but not much more from other victims," Cody said. "This Fairchild guy's ex-wife had tossed all his personal stuff out by the time I began to investigate his file."

"Well, I think I may be able to help you on this stretched fabric bit. My chum Paul and I were wrestling a big drunk guy into the back of our squad car last week. Paul had him by the back of his jacket, while I had his legs.

"The back of jacket, near the shoulder, just below the collar tore as Paul pulled him into the car. That fabric stretch marks and skin fragments are from your perp's fingers. The partial fingerprint may also lead to something, but I would take another look at the fabric," Jamie advised.

The jumper evidence was tested in December, eight months earlier. Cody wondered if new technology may have been developed since then. He would ask Neil about it right after lunch. The two men enjoyed their meal, while other cops came and went, some stopping to chat. Some looked at the spreadsheet and others just waited for their takeout order. None of them commented.

That was how investigations went. Little pieces of the puzzle fit, others didn't. The picture got clearer with each new piece put into place. What kept Cody awake at night, was all those pieces that didn't fit. He had to get a break soon.

The last five, who went missing all at once, motivated the Mayor to increase the investigation's budget to add personnel. He was worried about potential backlash from the Governor of Massachusetts and the adjoining states. He should have authorized more resources for the MPs case, back when the body count was confined to Boston's low-income neighborhoods. Now, it had spread to other states and the Mayor was understandably nervous. Bad publicity caused voters to react negatively against the incumbent at election time.

"Can you have a second look at the topcoat from the December University Bridge-jumper case? The stretched fabric may be the result of the perp pulling the victim into the back of the car. The formerly untestable skin fragments may now be testable," Cody said. He had to leave no stone unturned.

"Detective, you know we're up to our ass in alligators in this department. The Mayor may have given you more resources, but he sure as hell didn't let any spill onto our floor. We are three weeks behind as it is. Your fabric tests must get in line, unless you can get me more help," Neil said. He was frustrated with the lack of support his department was getting and he mulled the old case over before adding, "there was that partial thumb print. Did you send that to the FBI to be cross-referenced? They have lots of spare cash, they and Homeland. Hell, send them the topcoat too," Neil said in exasperation.

The shortage of funding in support departments of the Boston Police were on the verge of becoming critical. When Cody broached Neil's request for more help in the forensic lab, both the Captain and the Superintendent looked at each other and replied in unison, "That won't happen!"

Cody's next request got a totally unexpected response. He suggested sending the topcoat to the FBI for testing. The faces of both men became ashen and frown-lines knitted at their foreheads.

"We don't want the Feds taking over the MP's case. They have jurisdiction because the perp is now operating across state lines. If they get involved, the media will have a field day with the news right across the country. The impact on our tourism would be devastating. The Feds have left us alone so far because they are busy chasing the ghosts of international terrorists," the Superintendent said. "The last thing we want is to bring this case to their attention."

"I'll speak to the head of Forensics to see if I can pull a few strings," the Captain said, while the Superintendent nodded in agreement.

"If you don't mind, it might be best to leave sleeping dogs lie," Cody said. "The other detectives and I have a pretty good working relationship with the staff on the forensic floor. If you rattle their bosses' cage, it might interrupt the delicate balance that we have developed." It was not often a subordinate spoke so freely in front of his boss's supervisor, as Cody had just done. It showed the respect he had earned from both men in the past few years of working together.

"Is there anything else Cody?" the Captain asked.

"Only, that I am going to send a few city workers down into the storm drains around Newton Highlands. Those five new missing people could generate some blood evidence if it's our perp. I don't want to miss any leads I can find," Cody said.

"I approve that request. Just watch your budget and no more than 50 hours from the city crews and ten DNA lab tests. I'll inform Forensics to expect the extra workload, and to prioritize the water-testing analysis," Captain Evenly said.

Over the next week, with Arman's help, they tested sixty-seven catch basins around the Newton Highlands area. It was a shotgun-style effort, like throwing darts at a map and testing wherever they hit. Not a trace of blood showed up. The first blood test work Neil did, used the Hermastix system successfully. Cody acquired a small vial of the agent for field tests from Neil. Now they could just put a drop of the substance into a test-tube of drain water and have results instantly. They could only tell if there was blood contained in the sample water, so the lab would be needed to check those positive samples for human blood and DNA.

The crews reported the smell of laundry bleach in the water. It could be attributed to more people washing their cars in the summer. "Most laundry soaps contain bleach crystals," said Arman, the sewage water expert. "The bleach destroys the blood cells. It literally tears them to shreds and disrupts the Hermastix from working."

They had exceeded the Captain's budget ten-fold, without a shred of evidence to show for it. The only good news was that their budget for DNA testing was still in place. That Friday, Cody prepared his data and made ready for Monday morning's show and tell session.

Cody had been in contact with both Newburyport and Worcester, Massachusetts police departments. He wanted firsthand information from the investigating officers on these last missing person cases.

The Worcester detachment had determined that the last time the three missing people were seen, they were in the company of a well built, middle aged male. He was clean shaven and well dressed in his casual summer attire. Their server said he seemed to be well educated. His manners were polished, unlike the three-missing people. They had spent several hours drinking and talking in the Horseshoe Bar and Grill. The well-spoken one picked up the tab using a prepaid credit card and left her a good tip.

The Newburyport police reported that their two missing women were married to sailors. Both men were at sea when their wives went missing. It was odd that the last time they were seen was in the company of a dapper-looking gentleman. He was obviously from out of town because he showed them a brochure of his fancy hotel suite. They had left a copy of the brochure behind on the table. The waitress in the Piggy's Paw Lounge said they were a spirited trio, who danced with each other and had a good time. They drank for two hours or so. The women were clearly drunk, but the dapper Dan seemed sober. She noticed that he consumed a lot of food and frequented the toilet more often.

"Usually women use the john more than men but that wasn't the case with those three. They left together about 10:00 p.m., giggling like kids on their way to a carnival.

The investigating officer reported that both women were childless. They were bored while their husbands were at sea and had a reputation of flirting with other local women's husbands or boyfriends. They were good-looking women but it seemed they were not ladies.

Their names and information were added to Cody's spreadsheet. When his turn came the following Monday morning, he handed out his spreadsheet, printed on two, 11" x 18" sheets of paper. There were now 67 people missing. Thus far, he had little information on who took them, only that he knew it was a murder case. He also knew the crime was centered around the Newton Highlands area, a ten-block square of rural Boston.

The first comment from the gathering of police officers was from Detective Michaela Palmer, the officer Cody had lunch with at Topper's in December.

"Lieutenant, could these people be part of a cult who perhaps take ritual baths in human blood? That would explain the quantity of blood you found in the drain last month. There would be less blood from individual sacrificial rituals," she said.

"A few liters are not enough to bathe in."

Her comments started the flow of discussion. Cody and the Captain both took notes. They would share their collective information later. For now, they didn't want to break the rhythm of the discussion.

"That topcoat bothers me. Twice now, I found fingernail pieces in the fabric of people who had been beaten. When a fabric is grabbed hard enough to stretch it and leave skin traces, you can bet there's a broken fingernail embedded in the fabric," a fellow by the name of Peter said.

"If this is a cult and you can't find bodies, maybe they're kept as mementos in a big freezer, or something like that. You know when guys go up to Newfoundland to bag a moose, they store the meat in a commercial freezer. No one would question someone who shows up with wrapped meat every few days to put into their rental freezer locker," the officer said.

"I read a dispatch from Canada a few years back about a guy on a pig farm near Vancouver, BC who fed his animals with the chopped-up bodies of prostitutes. It took them what seemed like forever to catch the guy," the detective said.

After the session was over, Cody had just put the finishing touches on his spreadsheet, when his phone rang.

"Cody, this is Arman. Got a minute?" asked the voice of his friend at the city yard.

"Shoot, Arman, what's on your mind?"

"The guys were having coffee and you know how chatter goes. An idea was floated to use a 1.5-gallon sample of red colored water. There's a dye type on the market now that is totally bio-degradable and eco-friendly. The idea was to dump some in spots around the area in question, when the condition of 5% fluid-flow is present. It would act as a blood representative test similar to the conditions when we found the blood in June. They suggested you might even use animal blood if you choose to. It would work better. Either way, when you have a mixture of 1 to a 100 at the creek outfall, you would know approximately where the sample entered the storm drain system. Is that of any help to you?" he asked.

Cody had spent too much time with the Captain and his superiors lately. Some of the bureaucratic budgeting crap was beginning to rub off on him. The first thing that came out of his mouth was stupid and he knew it.

"What will it cost to do these tests?" He could have kicked himself for saying that. "Never mind that last question. The cost doesn't matter if the idea works. What do you think the chances of finding that needle in the haystack are, with this idea?" he asked.

"It's about fifty-fifty. I'd guess maybe a little better," Arman said.

"OK, thanks for letting me know. I'll think it over. Do you have the crew to do this extra work?" Cody asked.

"Yeah sure. We'll just report that we are doing flow tests to check for blockages in the system. We do those from time to time. It's standard procedure around here," Arman said.

"In that case, let's go for it! I would suggest you use animal blood if you can, that way you can test with Hermastix solution. When can you do it?" Cody asked.

"We will start as soon as the water flow drops to 5% flow rate, in a day or so. We can do one, maybe two tests at a time. If the weather holds, we can get most of the system checked in two weeks," Arman said.

Chapter 13

THE ORGAN MART

Sid was a very happy camper. Since Collin's departure from the hospital, the guy had worked like a dynamo. Sid asked for an organ and like an auto-parts supplier, it would be there within a few hours. Collin seemed to hold a corner on the supply market. He must have had sources from every hospital and morgue in the eastern USA. Since he no longer worked at the hospital, the supply of organs had improved, greatly.

When Collin told Sid that he had surplus organs, Sid sold them quickly on the black market. They had saved over a thousand lives since their startup last fall. Sid's offshore bank account had 2.7 million dollars on deposit, and he had sent Collin a similar amount.

The bone marrow produces a stem-cell blood that can be used in countless ways. Wherever organs and body parts needed to be rejuvenated, bone marrow blood was used. When injected into damaged tissue, new cells grew, and the damaged parts were restored.

The hair loss industry was experiencing an increased interest. Full scalp transplants were being done now. They followed the same procedure as a skin graft, and you could go swimming with the new hair within a few weeks of the operation.

Collin used more of each donor than ever before. His talents as a removal surgeon were improving daily. The more he did, the less waste he accumulated. Having five donors on the go at any one time, helped to streamline the procedure and to make it more efficient. The kiln was used to burn what little waste there was, once every two weeks. He kept the by-products of his unused donors in a chest freezer. When he had about 150 lbs., he would start up the kiln. He had reduced the unused body portions to just 12% of a cadaver by using these new salvaging methods.

Collin was in his garden that Saturday morning, digging in his evergreen hedge on Steven and Sylvia's side of his house, when young Joe Freeman rode his bike into the driveway. He tried his door clicker, which failed to open Collin's garage door. He smiled when the results proved the clicker didn't work. His friend Dr. MacDonald was a very smart guy and he liked him because he was kind.

"You changed the code, that's good," Joe said. "You can never be sure who might go in there. You could be robbed blind some night and never know it," he finished.

"What's new with you, everything OK at home?" Collin asked.

"Yeah, sure is, Dr. MacDonald. Things are cool." Joe was at an age where he was both child and adult. The hormones drove him like the wind chasing a dry leaf.

"What are you doing in the garden?" Joe asked.

"I'm digging in some ashes from my kiln. It's like little bits of clay powder, see." He put a small handful into Joe's palm. *The kid would freak if he knew it was human ashes,* Collin thought.

"Is it good for the garden?" Joe asked. He liked getting information from the doctor, who knew everything, and he was easy to talk to. Unlike some adults, such as his own dad. With him, it was "Do your homework and don't ask questions." Sometimes that was followed by a cuff on the back of his head. Dr. MacDonald took the time to explain things and he was nice.

"Sure is, well parts of it any way. It contains potassium and that helps regulate the plants' water balance. Ash is an alkaline that raises the PH level in the soil. Too much of it negatively affects the growth of bacteria and worms," Collin said.

"Is it acidic?" Joe asked. He was in in grade 8 at school and they were learning all about botany now.

"No. Just the opposite. Acidic soil is said to be a "0" and a very alkaline soil is a "14". What I'm aiming for is to get the soil around the tree's roots to about 7 or 8, that's when they grow best, and the foliage gets nice and green."

"You sure do know a lot of stuff, Dr. MacDonald. I'm going to stay in school to learn. Then I'm moving far away from here," Joe said. Collin could see the lad was hurting. It is hard to grow up without good parents. Collin's folks had died when he was in college and even then, it hurt, and he missed them.

"Want to dig some, Joe? There's an extra shovel over by the garage door," Collin said. The willing boy grabbed the shovel eagerly and started to bury the spade into the soil. "Stay between the trees and not too deep. You don't want to injure a root. If you cut the root, it's like cutting your toe and the root might get infected. That can lead to a very sick tree," Collin advised.

"I seen Mr. Wilson's cedar hedge. Every third tree is dead. Is that why? He cut a root?" Joe asked.

"I saw Mr. Wilson's trees," Collin corrected him. Before he could answer the boy's question, Joe blurted out his surprise.

"You saw them? Aren't they ugly, all brown like that?" Joe asked.

"Joe, I was trying to help you with your diction. It is correct to say you saw, not seen, Mr. Wilson's trees. As for your question, yes, it is possible he cut a root or dozens of other things that can infect a tree," Collin said.

It took no time at all before Joe was ready for a new adventure. His young mind chased thoughts and ideas like a pup chasing its tail.

"I got to go now. I'm supposed to play scrub baseball with the guys over at Hyde Playground." He dropped the shovel on the lawn and was on his bike. "Thanks, Dr. MacDonald, for everything. See you."

He was gone, as fast as he had come. Collin smiled to himself. To be 14 again... He didn't daydream often, but young Joe's enthusiasm was infectious. It had been twenty years since Collin had last played scrub baseball. He hummed "let's all go out to the ball game", as he finished up the yardwork. His neighbor Sylvia, who was watching from the bedroom window, thought to herself, he's getting better. It just takes time. That's what she had said to all her neighbors, "just give him time."

It was over a week later when Joe dropped by on one of his impromptu visits, like a bee looking for a flower to land on. For Joe, it was information he collected around the neighborhood. He sometimes carried news and more often, local gossip. Today the news was of a different nature.

"I had a dentist appointment and got the afternoon off school. I lied and told my mom the filling hurt but it really didn't. You know what I seen?" He stopped in mid-sentence and corrected himself. "You know what I saw? Some city workers dumping what looked like red paint down the catch basins. Not just once. but I seen…, I saw them do it twice this week and once last week. I asked what they were doing but they chased me away. What do you think they were doing?" the boy asked.

"I don't know. Maybe it was something to clean the storm drains with. It could be a disinfectant, like mercurochrome or iodine. They are both red, sort of," Collin said.

"If I see them myself, I will ask them. I'll tell them I'm a doctor, concerned about health issues," he said. "Just where did you see this happening?" he asked Joe.

"Over near Hyde park and near my school," Joe said.

"I have to go now to get more riverbank clay for my pottery work. I'll drive by that way and ask," Collin told the boy.

Collin knew very well what they were doing, looking for his clinic. He had heeded his daughter's warning about the blood a few months prior. Had someone seen the blood? He had been flushing with bleach the past while. Did the bleach disguise the blood sufficiently, he wondered? He resolved to stop allowing any blood or organic matter to escape down the drain in future. He would use the kiln to burn it. With the exhaust stack scrubber to clean the smoke it was virtually undetectable. He would only use the kiln late at night, after everyone in the neighborhood was asleep, just to be sure.

Befriending a young boy had possibly saved him from detection. *There was a God, even for us sinners*, Collin thought! Collin knew his daughter was an angel looking over him. He hoped she was with him tonight. He had three more fish to collect this evening because his supply was running low. Two were now just small parts in the ice chest and two more were going into the freezer tonight when he came home with more donors.

His heavy workload kept him swallowing pills, some to stop the ever-worsening twitch and some to help him sleep without his disturbing dreams. Then there were the Bennies to keep him awake on those long days when he had fresh donors in the clinic. His only social activity was the Tuesday night poker game, which he had to forego when he was busy. He wasn't drinking and for that, he was thankful, although the pills were getting out of hand. He had begun using strong opioids, such as Fentanyl, via **transdermal skin-patch delivery. It was steady and gradual.** Some days he needed two patches at once to calm his nerves.

Tonight, he was off to Wayland Middlesex County. It was a spread-out community, six by three miles in area with a population of 15,000 upper class farmers. Rich drunks were the easiest fish to catch. You didn't have to hook them with moneymaking schemes, just friendship and a little karaoke to soothe their frustrated souls. They even picked up the tab from time-to-time.

Collin was dressed as a businessman in his sports jacket and casual slacks. He had a neat, clean appearance when he entered the Thistle and Thorn Tavern at 5:30 pm, halfway through happy hour.

He had previously met these potential donors at this same bar in the past month. He had selected them because they all shared a common court date and presiding Judge. It was at his invitation via text message that they all met that evening for a celebration.

The first to arrive was Doris Fernery, a 29-year old African American girl, recently divorced and at loose ends. Next to arrive was Sharleen Baker the 35-year old, hardware store owner's wife. She was followed by a 32-year old, single dentist by the name of Charles Foreman.

All three had recently been charged with their third DUI and expected to receive a three to six-month jail sentence scheduled to start the next week. This would be their last hurrah before going to court the next day. They would have the privilege of wearing a radio ankle-bracelet for three days, while they settled their business affairs. There is nothing like being rich to get special privileges. A schnook off the street found guilty, would be behind bars before the Judge's gavel could hit the sound block.

These three would replenish Collin's supply of the blood types he needed to maintain the delivery of organs to his partner Sid Fournier. Sid had asked for a pair of type 0 negative lungs which Charles the dentist would supply. The other two would wait until a need for them arose. Sadly, Sharleen had started to smoke again. She had kicked the habit for two years, when Collin first met her. The stress of going to jail got her started again. It would very likely damage her lungs to the point where they would be poor transplant material.

In the past nine months, Collin had gained a wealth of information about the fish he trolled for. At the onset of a binge drinking session, they all exhibited the same symptoms. Drunks begin a binge drinking phase when they started having anxiety attacks and began to get the shakes after a full day of drinking. They are at odds with life and themselves. The Dopamine in their brain is a neurotransmitter that fails to support happy, reward motivated behavior. This failure to perform properly is due to excessive alcohol consumption.

The session always starts with a few drinks, to help them feel normal after a night of heavy alcohol consumption. They have every intention of continuing the day without additional alcohol. After the third pick-me-up drink, the addiction takes over and all thoughts of abstinence dissipate. They are in denial about their alcohol addiction and profess their ability to control their intake. They are the only ones who believed this lie. Their friends and family know only too well what will happen next.

The first part of the brain to be affected is the motor skills area and the trembling stops. A lack of judgement and morals follow. The area of the brain that controls memory slowly shuts down and the alcoholic cannot remember beyond that point. They say they can't recall what happened after they blackout. They consider this memory loss to be a normal part of life.

Shortly thereafter, they lose their sense of balance. The other bodily sensory systems, such as touch and hearing, begin to shut down. These sensors are not essential to drive a vehicle, which is usually when drunks leave for home in their car. They are now in the last remaining phase of consciousness.

As the binge drinking continues, the vocal cords, lips, tongue and motor skills begin to fail, causing the addict to slur their words. Eventually they become completely incoherent. Physical numbness develops and walking becomes a stagger. The eye/brain connection is interrupted, blurring their vision and causing bright lights to become painful.

Ask a drunk if he's sober and he will say, he most assuredly is. He denies having had more than a few. He seldom uses the word "drinks" in his vocabulary, and refers to them as his medicine, equalizers, pain killers or relaxers.

As more alcohol is consumed, the brain shuts down areas of the body and its organs that are not life supporting. At this phase, the brain is in a self-preservation mode. The drunk finally loses his sense of feeling, smell, hearing, speech, vision and mobility. If he is struck by a car as he staggers down the road, he will probably be found in the ditch passed-out but uninjured. The body's defense mechanism to this type of trauma is to relax and bend with the external forces. The body's survival mode at its finest, is activated. Vital organs such as the lungs breathe, the heart pumps and that is about the extent of what the alcohol-poisoned brain can accomplish.

The drinker at this stage, falls into a comatose-type sleep and no amount of external sound or movement will interrupt it. Once the liver and kidneys have had time to remove the excessive poison from the blood, he or she will then regain consciousness. The function of these two organs consumes a great deal of water to accomplish their work. Drunks awaken thirsty and physically exhausted. If they can remain alcohol-free after this re-awakening, the binge session will end.

This seldom happens because a binge drinker rarely passes out without some booze still left in the bottle. No matter how drunk they are, they will drink until they are physically unable to drink any more. Upon waking, they believe the pain will disappear with just one more drink.

The cycle starts again and can continue for days, until the body refuses to function. The drunk must then stop to dry out or die from alcohol poisoning. Few admit that they have an addiction or use the word "drunk" to describe themselves. It is at this stage that their family and friends abandon them. It is also at this point that

Collin draws them into his net. He then converts their useless lives into being productive organ donors.

"They say you can't smoke in jail anymore. I don't think I'll survive without being able to smoke," Sharleen said. She had been drinking Whiskey sours for over an hour and was beginning to slur her words.

All three fish expressed various stages of denial about what awaited them in the morning. Paul tried to cheer them up as they drank round after round. After his second drink, Paul switched to club soda and promised his small group that he would drive them all home safely when the bar closed. Tonight, was their night to drink up and enjoy. Since he would be their chauffeur, they drank with gusto.

By 11:30 the three amigos as they now called themselves were at the staggering, drunk stage. It was time for that one for the ditch and the ride home in Paul's car. Once again, Paul insisted they all use the toilet. He didn't want to search for a gas station during their ride home. It was then that he laced their drinks with GHB.

With the two women in the back seat and the dentist in the front they drove toward the hardware store and home for Sharleen. They were all asleep before they had driven even ten blocks. Collin diverted to his planned route home on Boston Post Road, I-20 east. When they arrived in his driveway about 12:30 a.m., all of Collin's neighbor's lights were out and they were asleep.

Collin was very efficient in handling the new arrivals. They were in their assigned ambulance gurneys and placed in proper order along the wall of his clinic. Blood and urine tests were completed and problems with any of their vital organs identified and recorded. All three were in a comatose state by 5:15 that morning, ready to donate their body parts.

Collin reveled in the notion that the sick and injured in the Boston area would reap the benefits of the fishes' donated organs. They had not even signed an organ-donor form. They had never considered the great public need for organs or those who had been caught up in a supply and demand quandary created by others. Nor did they ever suspect that they would be part of the solution through their generous, anonymous gifts.

Chapter 14

THE SEARCH CONTINUES

Detective Farnsworth couldn't believe his good luck. Armand's crew had narrowed down the likelihood of a blood source to a seven-block area. There were three cul-de-sacs within that area, a total of 150 homes and no businesses. It was time to enlist the Mayor's offer of extra funding to start canvassing door-to-door.

Cody and the Captain wanted the search done quickly so the culprits could not elude capture. It would be a one-day search. They sought peripheral information as a start, asking neighbors about odd activities. They would not ask if a resident had poured blood down their drain. It was to be a subtle canvas, done by students in their final weeks at the Police Academy. They would only ask questions of the adult residents and those questions would be non-threatening.

The students were to explain that they were on a training session from the academy. All answers were voluntary and would be kept confidential. The questions they asked were supplied by Cody and the police Captain. Had a resident seen or heard anything out of the ordinary in the past nine months? As an example, perhaps they could recall the activity of a neighbor at odd hours? Was there anyone in the neighborhood who was mentally ill or acting strangely? Was there anyone who they had noticed who was secretive or kept their blinds closed?

Inevitably, after the second question, people would become concerned. Was there a rapist in the area or perhaps a child molester or a pervert was on the loose? The junior police officers assured people that they were just practicing their investigative skills. There were no reported felons in the area to their knowledge, so the resident had no need to be concerned. Should a person require further calming they were to call upon the training officer for assistance. Should there still be concern after discussing the matter with the training officer, they were provided with Captain Evenly's business card for the citizen to call directly.

This was not normal procedure. To have a crew of trained officers canvas the same area would require days of legwork at great expense. The potential to scare off their quarry using the students as interviewers was minimal. The students were not to enter any homes, merely to ask the questions provided.

There was one trained officer for every nine students, who were dispatched in groups of three to interview each homeowner. If there were any concerns, the group leader was to signal the police officer, who would take over the interview.

When they hit Collin's cul-de-sac it was about 2:30 in the afternoon. The students got an earful from the neighbors in all seven areas they visited that day. The education they received would remain the highlight of their academy training and some responses garnered a smile or two.

"That lady over there, the house with blue trim on white, yes that one. She looks in my garbage every time I put it out for collection," one elderly man said.

"I think the man who lives over there is a drug addict. He smokes funny cigarettes that smell like perfume," one lady reported.

A few pointed to Dr. MacDonald's house as having strange activities late at night. No, he was just recovering from losing his family to a driving accident. He had behaved stand-offish at the block party two-months past and he makes pottery, of all things!

When the students gathered after the day's training session, they handed their reports in for Cody to review. He sat down with a hastily created spreadsheet to discuss the survey results with the three trained officers who had supervised the students that day.

Of the 150 homes they visited, three, stood out for further investigation. One was a Mr. Arthur Davis and his wife Jane, a retired couple. The elder man was seen digging in his back garden with a small flashlight attached to his forehead at night. The second was a Dr. Collin MacDonald and he was reported by seven of his neighbors as being a loose cannon at best and an out and out nutcase at worst. The third was a retired nurse who brought people into her home through the front door, but they were never seen to leave.

Cody did the standard background check on the three families interviewed by the students. The three came out clean as a whistle. None had even an unpaid parking ticket. The check did show that Collin MacDonald had suffered the loss of his family in an auto-accident the previous year. It involved a drunk driver who was released after being given a good lecture by the presiding judge.

Lieutenant Cody Farnsworth, in the company of Michaela Stevenson went to interview these three families in Newton Highlands the next day, on Tuesday. They chose the retired nurse as their first interview only because she was nearer to the highway then the other two. Following this logic, the retired couple, Mr. & Mrs. Davis would be their second visit.

* * *

Dr. MacDonald had also been busy since the three police students had landed on his doorstep. The meeting with the three had been pleasant on the surface but for Collin, it unfortunately spelled the end of his short-lived organ donor clinic.

As a man who was always ready for every eventuality, the invasion of his privacy was not unexpected. He knew without a doubt that the city workers were narrowing down on his location. Their work with the red dye placed in the catch basins the previous weeks had given him all the warning he needed. His daughter and young Joe's warnings had been all too clear.

He had his escape-plan organized and left that evening for the airport. Before leaving his home, Collin loosened the pipe union on the gas-supply line to his hot water tank. He blew out the pilot light, opened the doors to the recreation room and clinic, then closed all the windows in the house. He placed the hurricane door over the fireplace to prevent the lighter-than-air natural gas from escaping as it filled the house. Collin knew the gas would fill the house, from the roof and upper floors down to the basement. The air in the home would be mostly pushed out through the hot water tank chimney and the clothes dryer exhaust. It would take all night to totally fill the home and he set his escape plans in accordance to that time schedule.

He call-forwarded the front door security camera system to his burner cell phone, so he could see and speak to anyone coming to his door. He called Sid and brought him up to speed on the police action. He advised his friend that he had left the country and that Sid should cover his tracks. He was not in any danger if he suspended any further organ placements. Collin's last action before leaving for the airport, was to place a burner cell phone on the recreation room table, with a blasting cap connected to the phone's ringer.

He flew to Seattle under the name of Paul Mathews as a first-class passenger. His then destroyed all evidence of that persona. With his trail now erased, he stopped for the night at an I-5, Best Western Motel as Shane Mackenzie.

On Tuesday morning, sporting blonde hair and blue contact lenses, he used his new passport and ID, acquired from Sid's underworld friends to fly to Atlanta, Georgia. He used the credit cards he had acquired the month before in his new name, to cover his expenses. He would stay in Atlanta for the day, to complete his southern Caribbean travel plans. He only had to wait to receive a phone call from his home security system.

When he finished his preparations in Atlanta, it would only be a short flight to the Dominican Republic and freedom. Once there, Shane Mackenzie planned to purchase a ticket on an island clipper going further south. He would connect with a flight to Castries, the capital of the small island country of Saint Lucia, off the coast of Venezuela. The usual way for Americans to reach this southern island was via Caracas, the capital of Venezuela on the north coast. By using the costlier island-hopping flights, he hoped to foil any attempt to follow him.

There was one more disguise change in Saint Lucia to be secured…, cosmetic surgery to alter his nose and lip profile. An adjustment to the tissue around his eyes would complete his new face. The Foreign Office of this fine little country needed only his photo to issue a passport to Collin, in his new name, Dr. George Freeman.

He was now a blonde, blue-eyed physician with credentials that verified his six-year surgical studies at the Medical University of Martinique. Money can buy most things and these small island countries needed the income people like Collin offered.

* * *

Cody and Detective Michaela Stevenson approached the front door of the retired nurse, Miss Dorthey

Pickeered and rang the doorbell. A lady of about sixty answered the door and asked how she could help them. They looked like salespeople, and she was about to put the run on them.

"Good afternoon Miss Pickeered, I'm Detective Farnsworth and this is Detective Stevenson. May we come in for a few minutes, we have a few questions to ask you," Cody said.

"Is this anything to do with those young people that were here yesterday?" she asked.

"Yes, that's correct, we are doing a follow up," Michaela answered.

"Well they certainly got the neighborhood all in a tizzy. My goodness, I had people peeking out of their windows half the night watching to see if I might fly off on a witch's broom," Miss Pickeered said.

"Well I'm sorry for any inconvenience, ma'am," Cody said. "May we come inside and talk?" he asked again.

"Oh yes, I suppose so, come in," she said, after she had scrutinized their identification thoroughly. *"A lady must be cautious these days,"* she said to herself. The two detectives followed the lady into the living room and could see as they passed the dining area, it was converted into a cosmetic salon and massage parlor.

"Miss Pickeered, we are part of the Boston Police department's staff, investigating the disappearance of a number of people in the area. The student police were surveying the area for us and we are now conducting follow-up interviews. The student's interviews indicated that people arrive at your home but don't appear to leave. Can you explain the reason for this?" Cody asked.

"Well that's just silly. Those nosy neighbors are the cause of all this. My customers generally arrive by bus and after their massage and facial treatment I give them a ride back home. This is because their faces are quite red, and their vision is somewhat blurred after the treatment and sensitive to the air. They wear a protection cream that is obvious and unsightly to some folks. Once they get home, they put on the neutralizing cream and the redness goes away overnight. So, you see, it is just to help my customers, that is all," she said, "My car is parked in the back lane, so I guess those nosy neighbors don't see us leaving."

"Thank you, Miss Pickeered, for clearing this up for us. We will leave you now. Please accept our apologies for interrupting your day. We do have to follow up on any leads, no matter how trivial they may seem," Detective Michaela said.

Had the students the authority to dig a little deeper with their questioning techniques, they would have had the answer to Miss Pickeered's mystery. The two detectives left the home and checked the back lane. Sure enough, there was Miss Pickeered's car.

They then drove to the next cul-de-sac where the Davis's lived. At about 1:45 they rang the doorbell. Mrs. Davis answered and after a short introduction by the detectives, she invited them in.

"Arthur dear, there are two detectives here to see you," Jane called downstairs to her husband who was working in the tool room.

"Be sure to dust off before you come upstairs."

Turning back to the two police officers she said, "Come, this way officers. We can sit in the kitchen as Arthur will be dusty from his power tools."

When Arthur arrived, the four of them took seats at the kitchen table. It was a cozy room with the smell of fresh baked cookies in the air. Jane Davis offered coffee and cookies, but the two detectives declined. They just wanted to resolve the question of Arthur's digging in the back garden, late at night with a headlamp.

As Arthur sat down, the dust from the seat of his pants clouded out from the chair. His wife gave him a disapproving look and that put Arthur in a bad mood. These people interrupted his wood-working project. She should have sent them downstairs. Now she would fuss with cleaning the kitchen until suppertime. It was little wonder he kept busy with his numerous hobbies, just to stay out from being underfoot.

"What do you want? Has this anything to do with those idiots yesterday and their dumb survey? Can't you train your police students without disrupting the neighborhood?" he questioned.

"Mr. Davis, we are part of a task force looking for several missing persons. Yesterday's activities by the student police was to canvas the area and narrow down the field to a few people who might be able to help us with the investigation," Cody said.

"Have you seen any activities in the neighborhood that seem strange to you or your wife?" Michaela asked.

"That's what the kids were asking yesterday?" Arthur said. "Just cut the chaff. What the hell do you really want to ask me?" he asked.

"Now Arthur, don't be like that, these nice people are only doing their job," Jane said and turning to the detectives she asked, "Isn't that right, just doing your jobs, aren't you?"

Cody could see that Arthur was a man who liked to push his weight around if he could get away with it. Cody was also an alpha-male and his temper was rising. He would cut to the chaff, all right, the bastard deserved it.

"What is your reason for digging holes in your back yard at night? What are you burying out there that can't be done in the daylight?" Cody asked.

"Well, of all the dumb questions, that takes the cake. I have a garden full of containers growing African Night Crawlers. Those are worms, if you don't know it. I'm a verniculturist who has several hundred thousand lumbricus rubellus or simply named, red earthworms to feed. I produce nutrient-rich soil and organic fertilizer for garden shops and worms for fishing bait. Is there a law against that now?" he demanded.

"We would like to see this worm farm, if you don't mind," Michaela said.

"Why are you digging around in the bins at night?" she asked.

"Well it is my belief that you don't go exposing the nursery during the daylight hours. It causes trauma for the worms. If you want to dig around for body parts then you damn well can get a search warrant first," Arthur challenged.

"That won't be necessary, if I can see some worms and it all looks to be as you say," Cody replied. The exasperated man saw it would be better to cooperate, than resist.

"Alright, follow me and be sure not to step or fall into one of my bins." Arthur said. "I'll open one that's in the shade, but only for a few seconds, for you to have a look see."

The two detectives followed Mr. Davis out of the backdoor and down the steps into another world for the two police officers. Arthur lifted a four by eight-foot lid to one section of the nursery and hundreds of thousands of worms squiggled about. You could see where a new supply of rotting fruit and vegetation had been added. Their slimy-looking bodies wriggled through the muck, content to eat all that the farmer could supply.

Cody and Michaela's interest peaked, and Arthur sensed their attitude change. He mellowed substantially with the change in the officer's demeanor. He was now a true verniculturist and this was his domain. He showed them his composting bins filled with rotting fruit and vegetables collected from the local grocery stores.

"These insulated tarps over here are pulled out on cold nights. I must keep the nursery above 55 degrees Fahrenheit and below 80 degrees. They are insulated and one electric frost-fighter does the job most nights. If the worms get cold, they will roll into a ball like your fist with the other worms to keep warm. In the wintertime, they go deeper into the bins. These bins are two feet deep and four feet wide, by eight feet long. I get the equivalent of about a bin-full a month of soil to sell. Plus, perhaps a few hundred pounds of worms a month during the summer growing season," Arthur said.

"How many bins are out here in your backyard?" Michaela asked.

"My yard is 40' wide by 28' long. I need two feet between bins to service them. I have six rows of three bins each, which makes 24 bins with a twenty-five thousand worm capacity per bin. I harvest about 20,000 worms a day. That is about 20 pounds, every day. At $30 per lb., that's not bad scratch," Arthur said.

"Why do you have two types of worms, the African and red ones?" Michaela asked.

"They eat different types of food and have different breeding styles. I get better results with the reds over winter and the Africans breed fasted in summer. I just separate the citric fruit from the noncitric when I feed the different species," Arthur said.

As the detectives drove to their next interview at Dr. MacDonald's, one cul-de-sac south, Cody started the conversation with a rush of air escaping his lungs.

"Do you realize what that Arthur fellow is doing? He makes more money than a cannabis grower does with the same area of land. He does it legally too. The mob would go nuts with this kind of business plan. Can you imagine worm gardens scattered all over the city of Boston?" Cody asked and they both laughed.

"Yeah, gangsters, tending worm bins on every balcony. Couriers running one-pound bags of worms and dirt around the streets. It would turn into a shitty mess, right?" Michaela joked.

"OK, settle down, we're at the doctor's house. Look at the landscaping this guy has done. Those big tall cedar trees on both sides must have cost a fortune. How old do you think they are?" Cody asked.

"I'd guess maybe twenty-years, give or take. They certainly block off any view of the house from his neighbors, don't they?" Michaela replied.

Cody opened the file on their preliminary investigation of Dr. Collin MacDonald. He reviewed what they knew about the man, reading out loud for Michaela's benefit.

"It says here he survived a car crash that killed his entire family a year ago, last July. That would make him a hater of all the DUI persons on our missing persons list.

"He was an accomplished transplant surgeon at Mass. Hospital until he was released from his duties last March. It implies he was having a nervous breakdown but they covered it with proposing a brief period of absence so he could convalesce," Cody read. "It says here he never returned to work. His address fits nicely into the red dye flow-tests that Armando carried out. It also fits the general area of all the last seen locations," Cody continued.

"The one major connection is this guy's physical resemblance to that of Paul Mathews, who was stopped by the highway patrol officer. He drives a Lexus of the same color and the blood-test report said the missing woman had the same DNA as that found in the storm-drain," Cody finished.

"We should have brought a search warrant with us. This is the hottest lead we have on the case," Michaela said.

Getting out of the car, Cody said, "It only takes an hour to have someone bring a warrant out to us. Let's play it by ear and see where it goes. Maybe we will get lucky and the guy leads us to the alter he uses to worship his demons," Cody said.

He rang the doorbell and after 30 seconds, a male voice asked, "Who's there and how can I help you?"

"Is this the residence of Dr. Collin MacDonald, the surgeon?" Cody asked.

"It is. Who are you and what do you want?" the voice asked. Collin aka Shane Mackenzie sat in an airport waiting room at Gate 12, waiting to board a flight to Santa Domingo. The house security camera was patched to his burner cell phone in Atlanta, Georgia with an app he acquired for $20 a few weeks earlier.

"Dr. MacDonald, we have a few questions and hope you can help us resolve a few issues, that is all. May we come in and speak with you?" Michaela said in a soft, compassionate voice. *She has a voice that is dripping with honey*, Cody thought.

"I'm very sorry but I'm extremely busy with a load of pottery that I must get into my kiln in the next few minutes. I'll be five minutes. Would you mind waiting in your car, off my property for that long?" Collin's voice asked.

He could see the TV picture on his phone of the two police officers looking at each other. He couldn't make out what they whispered but their reply was affirmative, yes, they would wait.

"Only five minutes, sir," Cody said in a strong voice, "and then I apply for a search warrant."

Collin watched as the two walked to their car. He knew that only one would sit in the car, the other would go to the back lane to be sure he didn't escape that way. His timing at this point was critical. He didn't want to kill anyone. He was not a monster. He had compassion for his fellow man. That was why he ran such a fine organ-collection clinic.

While he watched on his cell phone, Michaela got out of the car and walked down the entrance street. He knew she would go to the back lane, a two-minute walk. He counted off 30 seconds to be sure she was safely away.

Then, with his other cell phone, he used the speed-dial to call the burner-phone connected to the blasting cap.

"All first-class passengers with preferred loading for Santa Domingo, please proceed to Gate 12. Thank you," came the voice over the airport speaker-system.

Collin saw the video picture on his cell phone blur and then go blank and he knew his family home was a pile of rubble. It was time to destroy the two burner phones and his connection to the USA. Collin aka **Shane Mackenzie boarded his pre-scheduled flight to the Dominican Republic.**

Lieutenant Farnsworth was the sole witness to the explosion that destroyed the MacDonald home that afternoon.

Michaela was over three-hundred-feet down the street and facing away. Cody sat in his car, watching out of the closed window with his car's air conditioner humming. He was deep in thought, going over the questions he was about to ask the doctor.

The natural gas from the leaking pipe union had slowly filled the entire house overnight, from top to bottom. As it rose to the upper floors, it entered every compartment of the home, filling every void it could find. It infiltrated the stud-framing and filled the voids in the insulation. There was not a cubic inch of the home that was not filled with natural gas, mixed with oxygenated air.

By early morning on Tuesday, it had reached the lower basement area. Every hollow space was filled. When the blasting cap responded to Collin's phone call, all hell itself, came to visit.

The lighter-than-air, natural-gas ignited and expanded many thousands of times its volume and the house were instantly reduced to a splintered pile of smoldering wood. Amazingly, the blast was contained by the large cedar trees on both property lines to the area on which the house once stood.

The debris rose high into the afternoon air and then fell back into the giant crater the explosion created. Every part of the house and its contents were now a pile of unrecognizable litter. Human body parts attached to blood circulating machines had become microscopic particles. It was a forensic nightmare, a jigsaw puzzle of monumental size.

Had the doctor committed suicide? Was he in this rubble? Cody and Michaela thought so. There was no DNA of his on file that they could use to compare it to.

The forensic tests on the topcoat was still not complete, although a fingernail had been found, embedded deep inside the wool fabric. Neil had indicated that a DNA extraction was possible.

In the weeks that followed, the cost of the investigation soared. Soon the Mayor's puppet, George was back in the Captain's office, complaining about the costs.

The experts had found fragments of what could be classed as a factory-like medical clinic in the basement of the house. There was sufficient body mass to create three complete bodies, although they represented seven different individuals, according to the DNA.

One of the many items found by the search team was the business card of a Sargent Warner Brierley. It was burnt and torn but the name was still legible.

By the third week after the explosion, a second explosion of a different sort occurred. This time it was sparked by the information on the fingernail DNA. It was not like any of the seven found in the doctor's house wreckage. This information told a story all on its own. Dr. Collin MacDonald's body was not in the wreckage. He had escaped the blast.

A search was made for an escape tunnel below the rubble in the basement area, but none was found. It was pure conjecture on the part of the police, about how the doctor had escaped the blast. The papers and TV news broadcasters had a field day with the story. Urban legends abounded and psychics came out of the woodwork with theories about aliens and poltergeists.

It was agreed between the police authorities and the politicians that the investigation would be suspended. Those 67-missing people were classed as possible victims of foul play by a person suspected to be the doctor. The case files would be placed in several banker boxes and stored with all the other cold-case files.

What nagged at Cody's gut was the flight to Seattle by a Paul Mathews. The trail went cold out west. After hundreds of hours spent scanning airport security films, they never turned up another picture of anyone of a similar profile or physique. It was as if a ghost had visited Boston that year.

The End

EPILOGUE

After spending a year sunning on the beaches of Saint Lucia, **Dr. George Freeman** applied for immigration to the USA. His desire was to move to Salem, Oregon to apply his much-needed skills as a surgeon.

He wrote the medical examination required by the state and waited patiently for months for the green card to be issued. Once in Oregon he went to work at Salem's Lady of Christ Hospital. He had to intern for a year until he was accepted as a practicing surgeon.

He soon moved to a larger hospital where he accepted a position as surgeon on the organ transplant floor. Within six months, his reputation for streamlining the transfer of living organs was becoming known around the world.

An offer to move to the city of Toronto, Canada as the Chief Medical Officer in charge of the Toronto Metro Hospital Transplant ward was being dangled before him. The organ transplant rules were less restrictive in Canada. They had a smaller population and were less politically controlled. The offer had merit and great potential for a doctor with his unique capabilities.

ABOUT THE AUTHOR

Kenneth Chamberlin began writing after he retired from his engineering and construction businesses. The Organ Thief is his sixth novel.

Kenneth has a military background, having served in the navy during the Cuban Missile Crisis where he suffered his hearing loss.

His many interests through-out the years include; flying, target shooting, hunting, sailing and designing gold processing plants.

The author lives on the west coast of Canada with his spouse of 24 years. You can contact Kenneth via email at:

kenbchamberlin@gmail.com

or visit his website at:

http://kennethchamberlin.wix.com/author

BOOKS BY

KENNETH CHAMBERLIN

Hidden in Plain Sight

Justice Best Served

Mega Thrust

The Galactic Ambassador

Cryonic Cyborgs

The Organ Thief

Broken Promises, Stolen Land

The Fall of Sentinel Hill

How to Kite into Retirement

Sky Tracker

The Spirit Wanderer

The Unflappable Mr. Brooks

Soldiering On

Made in the USA
Middletown, DE
11 October 2022

12514057R00144